SOLDIER DOGS

HEROES ON THE HOME FRONT

READ ALL THE

SOLDIER DOGS

BOOKS!

#1 AIR RAID SEARCH AND RESCUE

#2 ATTACK ON PEARL HARBOR

#3 SECRET MISSION: GUAM

#4 VICTORY AT NORMANDY

#5 BATTLE OF THE BULGE

SOLDIER DOGS

HEROES ON THE HOME FRONT

MARCUS SUTTER

ILLUSTRATIONS BY ANDIE TONG

HARPER FESTIVAL

An Imprint of HarperCollins*Publishers*

This book is dedicated to all the brave women of SPARS, who defended America's shores while the men in their lives served overseas. We will never forget.

HarperFestival is an imprint of HarperCollins Publishers.

Soldier Dogs #6: Heroes on the Home Front

For information address HarperCollins Children's Books, a division of HarperCollins Publishers, 195 Broadway, New York, NY 10007.
www.harpercollinschildrens.com
Library of Congress Control Number: 2019956223
ISBN 978-0-06-295797-9
Typography by Rick Farley
20 21 22 23 24 PC/LSCH 10 9 8 7 6 5 4 3 2 1

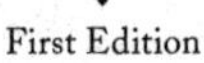

First Edition

PROLOGUE

JUNE 28, 1943
PALM BEACH, FLORIDA
10:31 P.M. LOCAL TIME

As the riptide pulled him out to sea, Charlie still couldn't believe the war had come to him. Right here, to his hometown.

He knew about what was happening across the world. The war was inescapable—every day on the radio, he'd heard reports of Hitler's march across Europe, through Poland and France. In newsreels at the local theater he'd seen how the Japanese had bombed Pearl Harbor, dragging the United States into this terrible world conflict. And even without the news, he saw the struggle every day on the streets. When he walked through the courtyard of his apartment building and saw the victory garden, when he strolled down the street and never encountered a man between eighteen and twenty-five.

Every minute he spent mourning Dad . . . that was part of it. The war existed in some shape or form for every moment of his life.

But he'd never dreamed it would be like this.

All around him bobbed pieces of burning wreckage, hunks of wood and metal. Huge slicks of flaming oil blazed along the surface of the water. His twin sister, Kate, shrieked his name and reached out for him from the end of a human chain, but no matter how hard he swam, Charlie couldn't reach her. Quite the opposite—with every second, the water pulled him farther and farther away. It was as if the sea were hungry and wanted Charlie for a snack.

A wave crashed over Charlie's head. Water filled his mouth, and he choked and coughed. He thought of Buster, his faithful dog, who'd been taken away by the coast guard for basic training. If only Buster were here now to help him. He couldn't believe the old boy was gone.

As his muscles grew tired and he found himself unable to keep treading water, Charlie thought that it made no sense that he would die in this war. He was only a kid! An *American* kid! From *Florida*! The war happened in London, and Paris, and Japan! Not here! Not America!

Another wave hit him in the face. He sank below the surface, swallowed by blackness.

CHAPTER 1

JUNE 12, 1943
OCEAN REEF PARK, FLORIDA
10:21 A.M. LOCAL TIME

"See anything?"

Charlie raised the binoculars back up to his eyes. By now, he was sweaty from the morning heat, and he felt the rubber padding squish against his face. He scanned the line of the beach, blazing white sand on top and brilliant blue water underneath. Other than a leathery-looking old couple in big hats strolling along the shore and a sandpiper speeding away from a crashing wave, it was empty.

Then, a blur of fur. A flash of sharp teeth. And—

"Buster, stop!" Charlie laughed, pushing the family Labrador retriever away. It was no use—Buster wanted attention, and Charlie knew that he wouldn't take no for an answer. Buster kept licking the lenses of the binoculars, and when Charlie pulled them away the big yellow Lab just moved forward and started licking his face. Charlie did his best to keep Buster off, but his resistance was half-hearted, and soon he was lying on his back in the scraggly grass, cackling as he tried to shield his face from the barrage of dog kisses.

"Careful," said Kate. She grabbed the binoculars away from him and wiped the lenses on the hem of her shirt.

"Ah, they'll be fine," said Charlie, finally pushing Buster off and climbing to his feet. He brushed sand and crabgrass from his butt and reached out to his twin sister, motioning for the binoculars. "Those were made by the navy. They're meant to take a beating."

Kate frowned and squinted into the distance;

Charlie had seen the look before, and he thought its underlying message was *that's not the point, dingus*.

"These were Dad's," mumbled Kate, and handed the binoculars back to him. "Be careful with them."

The words sent a wave of cold over Charlie that seemed to cut through the Florida heat. "I know," he said, but it felt like a small and silly response, like he was a little kid and not eleven years old. He took the binocs back and raised them to his eyes, trying to focus on the beach and not on how his sister's words made him feel. It's not like he was stupid. He knew why they were out there, watching the beach, same as they had for days. Because of Dad. Because he was gone.

"Anything?" said Kate.

"Nope," he sighed.

"Any balloon bombs?" she said. "Don't just watch the beach, look at the sky too."

"I said nothing," said Charlie, looking up in the air just in case.

At their feet, Buster whined. He trotted over to Kate and began winding between her legs. Kate bent down and petted him, whispering, "Calm down, Buster," but the dog couldn't stop moving.

His anxiousness only deepened the sadness in Charlie's heart. Dad was the only one who'd been able to get Buster to stay still for more than ten seconds. Now that he was gone, Buster was a nonstop blur.

After a few seconds, Kate sighed and turned back into the park.

"Come on," she said. "If there's nothing here, we should walk up the coast a bit to the beach. It'll tire Buster out too."

Charlie grabbed his backpack, and the two of them began walking north toward Ocean Reef Park. Up ahead, the morning's first sunbathers and swimmers had just set up on the white sand beach in front of one of the resorts. Charlie and Kate usually stuck to the park for U-boat watching—ever since Barry Thomas, the lifeguard at the resort farther north, had laughed at them in front of a bunch of tourists.

All Barry cared about was keeping people on the beach and in the resort. Not military work. Not the war.

These were Dad's. Charlie swallowed hard. He wasn't stupid. He knew the binocs had belonged to their father, and that they'd never get him back. Dad died when a U-boat—a Nazi submarine, famous for being silent and powerful—attacked his ship off the coast of Honduras. But just because Dad was gone didn't mean that he'd want the twins to treat all of his belongings like treasures they couldn't touch. Kate did that all the time, refusing to let Charlie handle Dad's stuff for long, always yelling that he had to be more careful. No one was allowed to sit in Dad's armchair in the living room. No one was allowed to listen to Dad's old radio.

Charlie frowned at the idea. He was allowed to use the binocs when and wherever he liked. Kate wasn't the boss of him.

Just to prove it to himself, he raised the binoculars to his eyes and stared out at the ocean.

He froze. A new, sharper wave of cold washed over him.

Was that . . .

"Kate," he said, grabbing his sister by the arm.

"Ouch! Hey, watch it." Kate saw Charlie

looking through the binocs and went quiet. "What is it? A U-boat?"

Charlie squinted and looked between the wriggling glimmers of light on the surface of the water. Had he just imagined it, or . . .

Two hands shot out of the water and waved. There, just audible over the sea breeze, he heard it:

"HELP!"

"It's a boy," said Charlie, lowering the binoculars and beginning to jog onto the hot sand of the beach. "He's drowning. Come on!"

CHAPTER 2

JUNE 12, 1943
PALM BEACH, FLORIDA
10:38 A.M. LOCAL TIME

Oh boy, running! Charlie was running! Buster launched into a full-on sprint. *He loved running! He could run faster than both of them! Look, a crab!*

Buster pounded the sand fast enough to get up in front of Charlie, and he immediately saw that something was wrong. The boy's face wasn't full of the grinning excitement Buster was used to. Instead, both he and Kate had the sharp, wide expressions of humans who were very afraid. Buster tried to be concerned for them, but the running had gotten him all riled up, and he found himself dancing back and forth in front of Charlie, trying to get his attention. What was going on? Was Charlie okay?

Why were they running? What was happening? Why were they scared? Buster wanted to play.

But something was wrong. Charlie and Kate were calling out to the other humans on the beach, their voices high-pitched and scared. The other humans came rushing over from their chairs and towels and looked out into the water. Was there something out there? Buster pranced in the surf and tried to see, but he couldn't make anything out. There were so many noises and smells here—radios and crashing waves and talking and shouting and those birds and that truck a block over and hot dogs. What was he supposed to do?

One by one, the humans joined hands. Charlie was at the front and began making his way into the water, creating some kind of leash made out of people with everyone else behind him.

Wait, was this . . . a *game*? Buster *loved* games! He barked and ran out into the water, splashing and paddling as hard as he could. He was supposed to get out in front of the last person on the human leash, right? They wanted to see how good a swimmer he was! He could swim so well! Charlie would be so proud of him!

Buster got out in front of the line and paddled over to Charlie. He began licking Charlie's face—but Charlie shoved him back hard and said some mean words.

From behind Charlie, he heard Kate yell for him to turn around in her loudest voice. Was this not the game?

Buster whined. The water was cool around him, and it smelled like salt, and fish, and good times. Why was Charlie splashing water at him instead of playing? Why was—

"HELP!"

Wait.

Buster heard the voice over the noise all around him, and he turned toward the open water.

There, in the distance, he heard it again. A human pup, out in the ocean, calling for help the way Charlie had done when he'd hurt his leg a while ago. He remembered that day—Dad was

there. They couldn't see Charlie, but they heard him somewhere in the distance. Dad had scratched his head and told him to go find Charlie.

Scratched his head . . .

Just like that, all the noises died out. All the smells went away.

Just like that, everything inside him clicked.

He paddled hard. He couldn't stop himself. The feeling—that same feeling, the feeling from the memory of Dad telling him to go find Charlie—drove him to the spot where the noise was coming from. There, up ahead, in the water, he saw the human pup. The boy was younger than Kate and Charlie, but not by much.

Buster's feet kicked harder beneath the surface. He surged through the water, intent on reaching the boy.

When he reached the human pup, Buster instantly felt the current in the water beneath them, pulling them farther out to sea. The boy must have gotten pulled out by it. He saw the panic in the boy's eyes and braced himself. Sure enough, when he was only a few feet away, the human pup splashed forward and threw his arms around Buster. Buster didn't love harsh handling, but he could feel the boy's pounding heart through his chest. If Buster had been any later . . .

Buster turned and paddled, but the water pulled at him. He could feel the way it grabbed at his fur—the more he tried to swim to the beach, the harder he was yanked out to sea. But if he didn't fight it, if he paddled to the side instead, the pull on his fur lessened and he could break the ocean's grip on him.

He put his snout down and worked his way to one side, sending drops of water spraying in the air where his nose met the ocean. Up ahead, he saw Charlie reaching out for him. He seemed to be getting farther away.

No. Buster growled, dragging the boy even harder. He could do this. He *had* to do this.

Almost there . . .

CHAPTER 3

JUNE 12, 1943
PALM BEACH, FLORIDA
10:48 A.M. LOCAL TIME

"Pull!" cried Charlie from the head of the line.

Kate dug her feet into the wet sand. Gave it her all. Felt her muscles strain. She pulled Charlie's hand, Barry the lifeguard pulled hers, the big older woman in the blue bathing suit pulled Barry, the bucktoothed kid in the sunglasses pulled the older woman, and bit by bit they dragged the human chain in, until Charlie and Buster came splashing out of the water, the dog helping the shivering, pale kid onto the shore.

"Is he okay?" cried Kate, breathing hard with both fear and exertion. She couldn't believe they'd just saved the boy. "Is he going to be all right?"

"He'll be fine," said Barry, brushing Charlie away and examining the shivering child. Buster tried to lick the boy's face, but Barry raised his hand as though to strike him, and the dog backed off. Kate glared at the teenager—of course he was the type to hit a defenseless animal.

The woman in the blue suit brought a beach towel, and the kid wrapped it tightly around himself. To Kate, he looked like two big, shiny eyes peeking out of a pile of cloth. Like a bad ghost costume on Halloween. Poor guy.

Barry patted his back. "What's your name, buddy?"

"J-J-Jeffrey," stammered the kid, shivering despite the heat.

"I saw him with our binoculars," said Charlie. He reached for the binoculars Kate had left sitting in the sand on shore. She snatched them up before he could grab them. What was Charlie doing? They were *Dad's.* He had to be *careful.* He could damage them. Not on her watch. Barry looked up at Charlie, then at Kate. His face curled into an ugly sneer. As always, his mind was on keeping the beach calm and his bosses at the resort happy. They'd saved this kid, but Barry just saw them as a nuisance. "I told you not to come around here looking for U-boats like a lunatic, Rankin. Scram."

"He just saved that boy's life, and you're telling him to scram?" snapped Kate. "Where were you? Isn't spotting drowning kids your *job*, Barry?"

The bystanders around them murmured agreement. Barry turned and loomed over Kate and Charlie. Charlie shrank back, but Kate stared right back up at him. Look at this noodle of a boy. Seventeen years old and acting like a grown-up because there weren't any other men around. She wasn't afraid.

"Listen up, buttercup," he said. "If you talk to me again like that, I'll—"

"Jeffrey!"

Kate looked up just in time to see a man drop his corn dog and ice cream cone as he sprinted across the beach. He brushed right past Barry and slid to a halt next to the little boy in the towel.

He was an older boy, she saw, his jaw square and his body tight with muscle. On his one shoulder blade were two scars, small and shiny, right next to each other. His physique and wounds told Kate he was in the military.

"Jeffrey, buddy, I'm so sorry," said the man, pulling the kid into a hug. He stood and turned around, suddenly making Barry look very small and scared. "What happened here? Is my little brother okay?"

"Sir, your brother got sucked out by the riptide," said Barry. "Thankfully, he was saved by—"

"The dog!" cried Jeffrey, pointing. "That dog saved my life! He dragged me in when no one else could reach me!"

All eyes followed his finger . . . to Buster, who was distracted in the surf. The yellow Lab had somehow found a horseshoe crab. He was tossing it into the air with his mouth while the creature's legs spun helplessly. Kate forced herself to swallow her laughter—she probably wouldn't find it funny if she were the horseshoe crab.

"Whose dog is that?" asked the older boy.

"Ours," she said quickly, holding up her hand.

To demonstrate, she yelled, "Buster, come!" Buster dropped the poor sea bug and trotted excitedly over to them. She hoped he would look heroic and professional; instead, he jumped up and put his sandy paws on her shirt. "Oh, yuck. Down, boy!"

The man laughed and sidestepped Barry to face the twins. "I like a dog like that," he said, sticking out his hand. "Wish I was more like him. Hank Collins, US Coast Guard. Pleasure to meet you two."

Kate shook his warm hand slowly. Oh boy, what was this? Her mouth was dry. She couldn't blink. This close, she could see Hank Collins's big brown eyes, his square jaw. The way he smiled at her made her feel like a candy bar in the sun. That was new.

When it was Charlie's turn, he raised an eyebrow at Kate and spoke for them. "I'm Charlie. This is my twin sister, Kate, she's . . . shy." Kate smiled politely. She could've socked him. "And this is Buster."

"Thanks, Buster," said Hank, kneeling down to pet the dog. Jeffrey came over, and the two scratched Buster around the neck. Buster, for his part, looked up at Kate with as stupid and tongue-lolling a face as she'd ever seen. She couldn't help but laugh—he wasn't a very complicated dog, but he was a good dog nonetheless.

"It's a good thing we saw you, kid," said Charlie, chucking Jeffrey on the shoulder. "Those riptides can be deadly."

Hank looked at the binoculars in Kate's hand and grinned. "Well, I'll be. Lucky you guys were keeping watch! What were you looking for?"

Charlie opened his mouth to speak, but before he could, Barry made a scoffing noise. "They come out here to look for U-boats from the shore," he said. "They're here every day. It's ridiculous."

"Our daddy died in a U-boat attack off of Honduras," blurted out Kate. Oh great. Everyone looked at her in silence. What was her problem?

"I'm sorry to hear that, Kate," said Hank. "I figure if my pop had died that way, I'd be out looking for U-boats too. Besides, there are naval battles going on closer to Florida than you might think." He shot Barry a dirty look and turned his attention to Buster. Then he did something strange—he started inspecting the dog. He turned Buster's head from side to side, lifted up his chop to look at his teeth, peered into his ears. Buster didn't seem to mind—his tongue hung out of his mouth, and his tail beat the wet sand of the beach as it wagged.

"Is everything okay with our dog, mister?" asked Charlie.

"Everything's great, actually," said Hank. A smile crept over his face. Kate liked the look of it. "Kids, I have a proposition for you. You hot dog kids, or more the popcorn type?"

Charlie looked at Kate. "Popcorn?" he said with a smile.

"10-4," she said.

CHAPTER 4

JUNE 12, 1943
PALM BEACH, FLORIDA
11:19 P.M. LOCAL TIME

Buster lay on the kitchen floor and whined to himself. Usually, the floor was cool and could calm him down. He could relax a little and not feel like a million things were running through his head at once. But he couldn't quite get comfortable tonight.

It had been a long day. First, he'd saved the human pup Jeffrey. Then they'd met the big man, Hank, who had been so nice to Buster and had pet him and given him a treat (a whole burger!), and had talked to Charlie and Kate for a while on the sand, saying his name over and over, *Buster, Buster* . . . as well as another word Buster had heard a lot lately.

War.

Hank had talked about *war.* Charlie and Kate had gotten sad. No, not just sad—excited, but also sad. Scared, maybe? They kept looking at Buster, like they did before they took him to the vet, or before they would try to give him a bath and he'd play a round of chase. They were a little scared, and a little upset, but also sort of happy. Happy about what they were hearing, but worried about what it meant. Worried about the *war.*

War. Buster didn't quite understand what it was, but he had an idea. It wasn't a word that was meant for him, not one of the human words that dogs knew by heart, like *sit* or *heel* or *don't* or *oh, Buster, what have you done?* It was a word the humans said to one another in a voice that made Buster think it was a big, scary animal that could come up and eat you at any moment. *War,* they'd say, as though they could see it in the distance and wanted to run if it got any closer. Buster wished he could get a smell for *war,* see what it looked like, so he could help protect the twins from it if it ever came sniffing around.

Buster huffed, got up, and walked around the apartment. Restless. He couldn't sleep, couldn't stop thinking.

Something was up. After they'd gotten home, Charlie and Kate had talked about him so much, but they wouldn't look at him. What did that mean?

He went to his nighttime spot.

He trotted to the armchair in the living room and laid down at one side of it. It was Buster's spot when Dad had still been around. When Dad came home, he would sit in that armchair, and Buster would sit there next to him. Every few minutes, Dad's hand would come down and find the top of Buster's head, and scratch it. Buster would have a moment then, like the moment he had today when he'd heard the human pup, where everything slowed down and lined up and he was ready for anything.

It had happened today, when he'd remembered Dad. It was the first time he'd thought of that moment . . . and the first time he'd felt like everything slowed down since Dad had gone away. He wished he knew how that had happened.

He knew it wasn't Dad. Dad was gone. Charlie and Kate and Mom had all gotten very sad for a long while. It had changed everything around the house. He'd laid here in his spot one afternoon, to try to get a little bit of Dad's smell, and when Mom had found him there she'd started crying, and she wouldn't stop no matter how much Buster licked her hands. Now, he only came here at night, when he could hear that everyone was asleep. And every night, Dad's smells were a little thinner when he came back. Soon, he knew, they'd be gone entirely.

He wished he knew what was going on. He wished he knew why Kate and Charlie were so scared and excited. Why they kept saying his name but not looking at him. He knew he wasn't always a good boy, that sometimes he didn't hear the *Sit* or *Stay* or at least didn't understand it. He knew that smells and sounds got so loud to him that he couldn't do what they wanted . . . but he tried. He hoped they weren't mad. He hoped they wouldn't send him away.

Buster put his head down. Closed his eyes, tried to stop thinking and sleep. Tried not to think about tomorrow, about the feeling he had that something big was coming, that he better get ready.

CHAPTER 5

JUNE 13, 1943
PALM BEACH, FLORIDA
6:56 A.M. LOCAL TIME

They told Mom in the morning. Charlie was nervous the entire time, while she leaned against the sink in her dark-blue blazer and skirt, listening to them. After Dad died, Mom had joined the Waves (Women Accepted for Volunteer Emergency Service—Kate described it as the navy for women, which, she always made a point of saying, the navy should be anyway). After that, Mom always had her uniform ready, and she never sat at the table with them. She said it was because she might get called to drive an ambulance at any moment. Kate was like that too—always looking for an answer, always wanting things to be neat and quick. Charlie wondered if both of them just felt weird sitting at their kitchen table without Dad.

Mom paused midway through her slice of toast. She brushed crumbs from her lips and frowned. "I don't understand. How could Buster help the war effort?"

Beneath the table, Buster, hearing his name, wagged his tail, making the whole table shake. Charlie looked down at the dog and sighed. He certainly wasn't doing a lot to prove to anyone that he was a smart, capable dog.

"Petty Officer Collins thinks he could do good work at sea," said Kate quickly. "He said they need strong swimmers who aren't afraid to jump right into the fight."

"And he said that the coast guard would do all the hard work," added Charlie. "They're going to train Buster and everything. So all we'd have to do is let them take care of him. It wouldn't cost us anything or take up any time."

"Guys . . . I don't know," said Mom. Her voice

bugged Charlie; it was the voice she used when she said *I'll think about it* and actually meant *No.* "When is this guy coming by? My shift starts soon."

"He should be—" Before Charlie could say anything else, the doorbell rang. Buster barked and scrambled for the door, his toenails clicking on the kitchen's linoleum floor. Less than a second later, Kate was on her feet and running after the dog.

Kate opened the door, and Hank walked in looking official in his blue coast guard jacket with its tight collar and nametag. Charlie thought he looked especially sharp and knew he'd make a good impression—and then Buster jumped up and put his dirty paws on him. Hank didn't seem to mind, laughing and petting Buster's ears and neck before lightly shoving him off and approaching Mom.

"Petty Officer Hank Collins," he said, taking off his hat and extending a hand. "You must be Mrs. Rankin."

"Samantha Rankin," she said, shaking his hand hard. "Medical corps."

"Yes, of course," said Hank, and saluted. "Pardon me, ma'am. We all appreciate how much Wave does for the home front." Charlie watched as Hank's charming smile changed into a tight look of hard respect. He saw that happen a lot to men when they spoke to her. Some of them thought her uniform was more costume than job. A few minutes into the conversation, they weren't so keen to call her "little lady" anymore.

Mom got Hank a cup of coffee, and he sat down at the kitchen table and explained his basic idea to her. Just like when the twins told her, Mom didn't seem to buy it.

"You want me to believe dogs are going to win this war for us?" she asked.

"Well, obviously it's not that simple," said Hank, sounding intimidated. Charlie could tell he'd planned to use a lot of charm and sweetness to win over their mother, but Sam Rankin wasn't about that. Since the war had started—and especially once Dad was gone—Mom had become no-nonsense, not allowing men to act like she should feel blessed just to get their attention. Charlie had seen the attitude rub off on Kate, too, who refused to let boys push her around—although, he noticed, Kate's eyes hadn't left Hank from the moment he'd walked in. To be fair, she looked more confused than happy about it.

"As you certainly know, the war at home is almost as tough as the war abroad," said Hank. "Especially for the coast guard along the eastern seaboard, where there are submarine battles going on only a few miles away. With the constant danger this situation creates, we need all the heroes we can get. And unlike people, dogs don't get caught up thinking about whether or not they might get hurt, or ruin their uniform, or what their personal politics are. Yesterday, Buster jumped in the ocean and saved my brother without a moment's hesitation. That kind of help is invaluable to us in the program I'm working with."

"He was really brave, Mom," said Kate. "Weren't you, Buster? Who was a brave guy?"

Buster jumped around excitedly at the mention of his name. Mom smiled at him, and Charlie thought he could see her guard start to crack just a tiny bit. But then she sighed and looked down at her hands.

"Officer Collins, we all love Buster, just as my husband did," she said calmly. "But he's . . . a distractible dog. He gets into the garbage and chases crabs for miles. One time, he disappeared for three days. So while I appreciate that he did something very noble yesterday, I wonder if you're not . . ." A sad smile crept across her face. "Barking up the wrong tree."

"Mrs. Rankin, I've worked with bad dogs in the past," said Hank. "Dogs way more excitable than Buster. That's the point of our training program—to get him into shape. Buster already has a huge heart, and that's honestly fifty percent of the job here. Giving him the know-how will be easy."

Mom looked at Buster. Charlie could tell she wasn't just thinking about the dog—she was thinking about Dad, the war, everything it had done to their lives. Charlie hoped she'd say yes. The thought of Buster being part of the war effort—of him and Kate patrolling the beach with their trained coast guard dog flanking them—made him swell with pride.

"How long would training be?" asked Mom.

Charlie and Kate's eyes met. Their mouths

curled into smiles. It had worked. Buster would become a soldier.

"A few weeks," said Hank. "I'm leaving for Virginia tomorrow, so I'd take Buster with me first thing in the morning."

Charlie's heart sank. He and Kate both lost their smiles instantly.

"Virginia?" asked Kate. "The training camp's not in Florida?"

"No," said Hank. "We'd be working at a base outside of Norfolk, a converted farm where we train lots of our animals. I'm just here visiting my family and scouting prospects." He grimaced. "Sorry, guys, I thought I told you."

"But . . . when would Buster come back?" asked Charlie.

"I'm not sure," said Hank. "But I'll level with you, Charlie—there's a great chance he might not. This is dangerous work, and dogs get assigned to all sorts of jobs across the country, sometimes even around the world. If Buster comes with me, he's probably coming with me for good."

Charlie looked down at Buster. The dog wagged his tail and put his head on Charlie's

knee. Charlie looked up and saw that his sister had the same blank expression as he did. They hadn't expected this.

They had a decision to make: keep Buster from maybe doing something great for the war effort . . . or never see him again.

CHAPTER 6

JUNE 14, 1943
PALM BEACH, FLORIDA
8:12 A.M. LOCAL TIME

Oh boy, they were going somewhere! Why were Charlie and Kate so quiet? They must be keeping it a secret, like they did with the dump that one time! Where were they going?

Buster couldn't hold still as Kate put the leash on him. He was always excited to go outside and run around, but something about today felt really special! The twins and Mom had been so quiet all morning, saying his name over and over, and at first he thought they might be going to the vet, which made him want to run and hide under the table.

But then he thought about it, and he realized that everyone did the opposite when they went to the vet—they laughed and acted fun and tried to get Buster to run alongside them, until they tricked him into running into the waiting room with all the other dogs and that cat with the one eye. So maybe it was the opposite of the vet! What could that be? Today might be exciting!

The minute Kate had him on the leash, he ran for the door. The door was closed. He wanted to go out. How could this happen? He whined as Kate waited for Charlie to put on his shoes. He could smell a truck outside! *Why* was the door closed?

Charlie opened the door, and a million smells and sounds blew in. Buster sprinted forward. He felt the leash go tight, heard Kate say, "*Whoa,* easy, Buster." He tried to calm down, be *easy*, but he couldn't, hearing the crashing surf, smelling the food cooking at the restaurant next door, bicycle bells, beach umbrellas, seaweed, asphalt, *EVERYTHING*!

Kate and Charlie finally finished locking up, and then they were off! Buster pulled Kate along, sniffing an endless parade of new scents as he walked, from freshly polished shoes on the building's steps to a lizard hiding in the plants outside their building. The day was bright, the world was loud and full of things, and Buster felt something, something powerful inside him that told him this was going to be a good day! The best day!

They walked Buster south, through the streets and away from the beach the twins liked to go to when they wanted to watch the water. Buster wondered where they were headed. He sniffed a trash can. What was with the twins? They were being awfully quiet, even for them. It almost felt like they were sad. How could they be, on such a beautiful day? He spotted an old food wrapper. Anything in it? No. How long would they be walking? The suspense was killing him!

Buster heard a voice and looked up. It was Hank! He sprinted, and this time Kate let him go, and he ran down the sidewalk to where Hank stood next to the human pup Jeffrey, the one Buster had saved in the water. What were *they* doing here? Buster leaped up on Hank, and the big human laughed and patted him around the ears. Then Buster gave Jeffrey a lick on the face, and the little boy giggled. This would be a fun day; he was sure of it!

Buster turned back to Charlie and Kate.

Why were they walking so slowly?

Then he saw their faces.

Wait.

Something was wrong.

He felt Hank's hand take the leash dangling from his neck. Jeffrey pet him a few times and made a shushing noise.

Charlie and Kate stood over Buster. They said some human words to Hank, and he said a few back. Buster could only understand a few of them, and even then, the feeling that something was wrong, and this would be bad, sent his mind racing. He looked from Hank to Charlie and back again. What was happening?

Charlie got down on his knees and held Buster's face in his hands. Tears ran down his cheeks, and he bit his lips between his teeth. Why was he crying? Buster leaned forward and licked a tear from his cheek, and Charlie laughed a little and pushed him away.

"Be good, Buster," said Charlie.

Buster didn't understand. Of course he was good. Charlie already knew that. Why would he say that? Buster looked to Kate, but she was also crying. She had her hand over her mouth, but Buster could hear it. Why? Kate was the strong one, with all the plans and the rules. What could make her cry? He went to nuzzle her hand, and she shook her head and turned away.

"Come on, Buster," said Hank, leading him away by his leash.

What was going on? Buster walked with Hank. Hank liked him—did Hank have the surprise? Were Charlie and Kate coming? *Ooh, the back of a car!* The seats felt nice under his paws. *Mmm, leather smell!* Huh, Hank closed the door. Where were Charlie and Kate? Wait, they were getting in one of the front seats. No, that was Hank again, now with Jeffrey. What was—

The car rumbled under Buster. He felt it begin to move.

Wait. No.

Buster turned to the back window of the car. Charlie and Kate grew smaller and smaller in

U.S
U.S.

his vision. They were holding each other, crying. What was happening?

Buster barked and whined. *Charlie! Kate! Come back!* Where were they taking him?

From up front, Hank shushed him, and said, "I know, Buster. I know, good boy." But Buster didn't know what to do or think. He just watched his family, his Charlie and his Kate, who had just given him away, as they got so small that they disappeared entirely.

CHAPTER 7

JUNE 24, 1943
PALM BEACH, FLORIDA
10:20 A.M. LOCAL TIME

Kate rapped her knuckles against the bedroom door. No answer.

"Charlie?" she said softly.

Still nothing.

Kate sighed and pinched the bridge of her nose. No progress. Maybe she should just leave him alone. She hated the idea. You didn't leave your friends behind. He'd been like this for over a week, ever since they'd handed Buster over to Hank—he just went into their bedroom, closed the door, and lay down on his bed. He only came out for meals, and even then, he barely ate. She'd had to patrol the beach by herself looking for U-boats, and it had been boring . . . and lonely. She had to admit that. Charlie was her twin. Her other half. Looking for U-boats by her lonesome just felt wrong.

She thought back on watching Buster drive away in Hank's car. She felt her own eyes sting. It wasn't like *her* heart hadn't gotten ripped out by it too. Buster wasn't just Charlie's dog, he belonged to the whole family. He'd been Dad's dog, after all. She bit her lip as she remembered Dad running down the block with Buster as a puppy trotting beside him, or sitting in his chair and scratching the top of Buster's head—

Wait. No. Kate clenched her eyes hard, wiped at the tears beginning to build in them. They had to make do with what little of Dad they had left. His things. His memories. The family. She couldn't think too hard about how he was gone. Mom had done the same thing after she'd heard the news—she'd toughened up, joined the Waves, started doing what she could to help her country and support her kids. There was no time to just be sad. Kate had to be strong.

She opened the door and walked inside. Their bedroom was shadowy blue, lit only by the sun coming in from under the blinds. Charlie lay on his bed, turned toward the wall. She came up behind him and nudged his shoulder, and he flinched away angrily.

"Rise and shine, sailor," said Kate. "Time to face another day."

"Go 'way, Kate," mumbled Charlie.

"Come on, Charlie," she said. "We have a job to do. There could be Nazis out there in the water, like the ones who got Dad. We need to keep an eye out for them."

"It won't be any fun without Buster," said Charlie, and he pulled his knees to his chest.

"It's not supposed to be *fun*," she said. "It's our duty as Americans."

Charlie didn't budge. Kate sat down on the bed and huffed. What could she do? Mom and Kate and all of the other women around Palm Beach had rolled up their sleeves and met the call while all the men were at war. But Charlie just kept acting so careless. Like with how he handled

Dad's things, especially his binoculars. What did he think this was, just another summer vacation? Was life one long shore leave to him?

Well . . . the more she thought about it, the more Kate's anger melted away. It *was* summer vacation, after all. Ever since school had ended, they'd spent every morning out at the beach, looking for U-boats or balloon bombs. Even officers like Hank got a day off once in a while, or he wouldn't have been at the beach buying his brother a snack. Besides, the more Kate thought about it, she was exhausted too—maybe not physically, but mentally. And maybe emotionally. Giving Buster away had been hard.

Was she being *too* tough? What did she and Charlie really need today?

"Ice cream?" she said.

Charlie shifted. "Huh?"

"Want to go get ice cream?" she said. She thought it sounded silly, not nearly as important as walking the beach . . . but it *was* tempting, and Charlie needed a break. "Mom left us a little change. We could go down to that stand on the beach with the soft serve and get a couple of cones." Wow, that actually sounded pretty great, now that she thought about it. Treats were a rare thing with the war on, but living in a hot town with resort beaches, they could at least count on a cone here or there.

Charlie was still . . . and then he rolled over, sat up, and wiped his eyes with the backs of his hands.

"I could eat," he said.

Charlie grabbed the change from Mom's jar by the door. They headed out of the apartment—Kate locked up after them—and through the cool cement halls of their building, until they came blasting out into the hot afternoon sun of the courtyard.

In the courtyard, Mr. Hornby was tending the building's victory garden, planted by the tenants to grow extra food to aid the war effort. He was a chubby older man with a gray mustache and veiny chicken legs coming out of his shorts. He waved and gave them a big, cheesy smile as they walked by him.

"Good morning, young friends!" he said. His weird accent came out hard on that one. Kate always noticed it. A little deep on the *R*s, a little long on the vowels. *Gud maw-nin, young frands.* New England, maybe?

"Hi, Mr. Hornby," said Charlie. "The garden looks really nice today."

"Ah, well, we must always try to make things grow beautifully," said the older man. He thumbed sweat from his brow. "The peppers will be especially good this summer. What about you two? Another day down at the beach, huh? If you ever get bored, you can always come tend the garden here with me!"

Kate tried not to roll her eyes. Dad had always liked Mr. Hornby, but he was a real goober. Charlie called him *Mr. Cornby* sometimes, because he was so corny.

"Maybe soon!" she said, and quickly ushered them out of the gate. They couldn't get sucked in. Ice cream over tomatoes, every time.

Kate focused on the sun on her face and tried, for once, to not think about the war. It was harder to do than she thought. Everything around them was a reminder of the constant struggle the whole country was facing right now. A blackout poster hung on the wall of their building. "WAIT FOR DAYLIGHT! The last hours of the blackout are as important as the first!" it exclaimed, featuring a frightened-looking rooster crowing—a warning to keep the windows dark at night so enemy planes and ships couldn't see the shore.

The smoke from a merchant marine vessel drifted lazily in the sky, off toward the beach. Even the people on the street were a reminder—as they walked, all they passed were women, kids, and old people. Any man between the ages of eighteen and thirty was either in Europe or out at sea, fighting the Nazis, Italians, and Japanese.

She wondered how Charlie did it—ignored it all and just let himself be sad about Buster. But maybe he wasn't ignoring it. Maybe the fact that it was everywhere weighed on him too. What if *that's* why she was so tired—

"Kate, watch out!" said Charlie. She felt his hand on her shoulder, pulling her back from the curb—just before a gray military truck drove past them, honking. Kate felt a surge of excitement and relief as she stepped back next to her brother.

"Thanks," she said with a shaky laugh, trying

not to show how rattled she was. "That was a close one."

But Charlie didn't respond—his eyes were pinned on the back of the truck. Kate followed them, past the tarp over the top and into the darkness beneath.

Hunched men. Striped uniforms. Shackles. Short blond hair, bright eyes full of anger.

"POWs," whispered Charlie, spelling it out—*pee oh double-yoos*, short for "prisoners of war." "Germans. Must be bringing them in from the camp in Tampa for work detail."

Kate felt a spark in the air, a ripple of energy. Just like that, it looked like old Charlie was back . . . but she didn't want to push him. Mom had taught her that—to use her head and make sure she knew the situation before taking action.

"What do you want to do?" she asked. "We could still get ice cream . . ."

Charlie looked at her, glanced out toward the beach . . . and then waved Kate in the direction of the truck. "Come on," he said. "Ice cream can wait. Buster would want us to follow them."

CHAPTER 8

JUNE 24, 1943
NORFOLK, VIRGINIA
10:42 A.M. LOCAL TIME

Grass!

Buster darted out onto the lawn and leaped in the air. This was incredible! There was so much sun, and so many smells, and hills in the distance, and fences, and bees, and dandelions, and *grass*, so much grass that he couldn't help but plunge face-first into it and roll around on his back in it, and then he even ate some, and boy, that was a bad idea, but who cared, because grass, air, *the country*!

Buster jumped up to see Hank and the two

other humans he came with. Hank and the one with the big round belly, Roy, were nice. They'd put their hands on Buster and hushed him while he was missing Charlie and Kate, and when the plane had scared him and he'd kept trying to stand up. The other, the skinny short-haired one, Nico, was mean. He stared down his face at Buster and crossed his arms. Buster could tell he was the kind of human who'd give you a kick for spilling a little water or something like that.

Hank whistled, and Buster came over and licked his hands. Were they going for a walk? Where was this place? Someone was cutting an onion somewhere. Could Buster run around wherever he wanted? If only Charlie and Kate were here! He bet they'd have so much fun in the grass. Maybe they could come and visit him!

"Easy, Buster, easy," said Hank, rubbing Buster's neck. Then Nico said something under his breath, and Roy shot him an angry look. Buster must be doing something bad. He didn't know what. He couldn't help it! He was so excited!

Hank snapped a leash onto Buster's collar and walked him through the property. There was so much to see—fences and sheds and buildings full of food and guns. A line of soldiers ran past them, and Buster tried to run with them, but Hank kept pulling him along. There was a garden and some kind of strange obstacle course, and then a pen with, whoa, were those horses? They were! He could smell their hooves and the hay they ate, just like those police officers back at home who rode them on the beach! One of the police officers had patted Buster on the head once. But the horse hadn't liked him. Ooh, that shed smelled like chemicals, the kind he could smell around the police! What was—

"Here, Buster," said Hank, and pulled him into a small building. Buster wondered what was going on here—and then he smelled one smell, and one only: *dog*.

There were other dogs here! Each of them with their own little kennel and bed and water dish! Buster launched forward at the first one, a girl dog kind of like him but with a lot of long, flowing fur around her face and ears! The collar bit into his neck as Hank edged him forward, saying, "Easy, easy." He sniffed her and whined at the girl dog, and she looked up at the humans like she wished they hadn't ruined her day.

"Buster," said Hank, "Daisy."

Buster danced around, whimpering and trying to say hi to Daisy, and to sniff her, but the other dog turned her face away and laid down on her cushion.

Hank pulled Buster out of Daisy's kennel and led him to the next one. Inside was another dog, small and long, with a pointed little face. Buster darted forward to exchange sniffs, but the small dog took a step away from him and made a low growl in his throat.

"Buster," said Hank, "Freddy."

Buster huffed at Freddy, tried to say hi, meet the dog properly, but the growl grew in volume, and Buster finally backed off. Wow, what was with these dogs? It's like they'd never played in the sand before. What had they been doing this whole time—

Hank led him to the third kennel in the corner. This one was kind of dark, and had a line of shiny pieces of metal that hung along the back wall.

"Buster," he said, "Skipper."

Hard eyes glared at Buster out of the shadows. He froze.

The dog who walked toward Buster was the same kind of dog as him, except a girl, and . . . *hard*. Not mean, but *strong*. Something about her smell, and the way she stood, and how she looked at him, told him that this dog didn't want to play. She was a serious dog. Strong eyebrows. Big muscles. Buster had seen dogs like her around the police officers and firefighters back in Florida. They had jobs. They meant business.

Skipper looked at him and huffed. Buster whimpered back. He looked the dog over and noticed a line in the fur down one of her legs. Oh, she'd been hurt! That was a hurt dog mark! Buster had one, too, from when he'd gotten tangled in a fence and had been cut. He stepped forward, sniffed at the wound—

Skipper stepped back and woofed. Buster didn't get it—did she not want to exchange smells? Maybe this was a game. He darted at her a little faster, put his nose down—

Skipper barked loud. She showed her teeth.

All of her muscles seemed to tense up.

He ran.

For a second, he felt the tug of Hank holding onto the leash, but then he was free, running out of the building and into the light. Everything flashed past him.

There were voices. He looked up. Roy and Nico crouched, like Charlie and Kate when he'd stolen a shoe. But they weren't playing. Buster backed up against a fencepost and whined. That dog had been scary! He'd never be as tough as that dog! Why did those other dogs hate him? He didn't do anything! There were too many smells here! He wanted to go home! Buster was a good dog! Buster was—

A scratch on the top of his head.

Buster felt his heartbeat slow down. Felt everything come into focus. It was okay. He was okay.

He looked up for the human who was giving him the scratch—only it wasn't a human, it was a horse! He was a big old guy, with a shaggy mane and spots of white around his hooves. The animal had leaned down and given Buster a scratch on the head with its big lips, like a little nibble.

The horse looked down at him with his big, dark eyes, and Buster thought he saw something like understanding there. Something like the way Dad used to look at him when he got all riled up. Buster barked and gave the horse a lick on the nose. It snorted and shook its head but didn't seem to mind all that much.

As the humans closed around him and he felt a hand tug at his collar, Buster kept his eyes on the horse until the very last second.

At least he'd made one friend.

CHAPTER 9

JUNE 24, 1943
PALM BEACH, FLORIDA
11:12 A.M. LOCAL TIME

The twins peered over the concrete roadside barrier and watched as the prisoners worked along the asphalt. As far as Charlie could tell, the POWs' job was to install fencing separating Route 1 from the barren sections of scraggly grass and sand leading to the beachfront. Some men dug holes for posts, while others assembled signs and poles, or unrolled and prepared chain-link fencing. They looked hot, thought Charlie; their arms and brows glistening with sweat in the afternoon heat as they trundled around in their heavy striped uniforms.

Charlie squinted. If only they'd brought the binoculars! Nuts on him for being so broken up about Buster!

"This part of the road is barely paved," said Charlie. "Why have them work all the way out here? There are probably sections closer to town that need repairing."

"I've heard they don't like civilians seeing them," whispered Kate. "People don't want to think about the enemy walking around on American soil, even as prisoners." She narrowed her eyes. "I don't see any cuffs or shackles. Why don't they run?"

"They wouldn't get far," said Charlie. He pointed to the back of the prison truck, where two Sheriff's Department officers with rifles sat and watched over the crew. And yet . . . Charlie noticed that when the occasional prisoner walked up to the guards to get a ladleful of water from their bucket, the two exchanged words, and the guards laughed. Some of the guards even called the prisoners by name. It looked like the Germans and the guards were friendlier than Charlie would've thought.

Charlie and Kate watched for a while longer, but there didn't seem to be much else going on—the prisoners dug holes, stuck in fence posts or signs, and rolled fencing between them. Charlie didn't like the fact that men who might have killed his dad could just walk around in America, but it wasn't as though they were being treated *that* humanely. They must be losing five pounds a day, sweating in those heavy uniforms. Maybe he and Kate should just go get their ice cream after all.

He was about to tell Kate they should sneak away and head back to the beach when he heard the ring of a bike bell.

In the wavering heat coming off of the road, Charlie saw only a blur at first, but as it got closer he picked out a shape—Miss Feng, their history teacher, rode her bike toward them. From the looks of the blanket-wrapped bundle in the front basket of her bike, she was on her way to the beach, probably for a picnic. Charlie never thought of her as anything other than an intense nuisance during the year, but seeing her riding along in summer clothes, he realized that she was just a person like anyone else. He even had to admit that she looked really pretty. . . .

Apparently, the prisoners thought so too—they all took a moment to stop and whistle or hoot at her as she rode by. Charlie felt Kate bristle at his side.

Miss Feng turned up her nose and swerved her bike to the far side of the road, close to their barrier—but before she could pass them, one of the guards, a tall man with a big gut and sunglasses, stepped out in front of her and put his hand up. Miss Feng skidded to a halt.

"Can I help you, Officer?" she asked in a hard voice that Charlie remembered from World History. He'd heard it more than once before. *Mr. Rankin, there better be a good explanation for this whoopee cushion.*

"Well, now, little lady, I sure hope so." The guard laughed. "Deputy Oliver Jacobs, at your service. Friends call me Ollie. Just wanted to make sure you have your ID on you. Not sure I've ever seen you around these parts."

Miss Feng reached into her bike basket, found

her handbag, and fished out her ID. Deputy Jacobs took it but barely looked at it. Charlie felt his face burn as anger swept over him. What a total creep this guy was.

"*Feng*, huh?" he said with a smirk. He even said the name wrong—Charlie knew it was pronounced *fung*, but the guard said *fang*, like what Dracula had. "You're not, heh, on your way to any sort of secret meetings, are you—" He checked the ID. "Leslie? Not passing any information on to Emperor Hirohito, right?"

"You're thinking of the Imperial Japanese Army," said Miss Feng flatly. "I'm Chinese. It's a common mistake among men who stop me on the street for no reason. May I go now?"

"Easy there, sweetheart," said Deputy Jacobs. "You wouldn't want me to have to get you a uniform and put you to work, would you?"

"Fraulein, we'll make you feel right at home on the line!" called out one of the prisoners. He spit in his hand and slicked his hair back. The guards and other prisoners chuckled. Miss Feng wrinkled up her nose and looked away.

Before Charlie knew it, Kate was over the

barrier and marching toward the guard. He barely had enough time to climb the concrete wedge himself before she yelled, "HEY," making Deputy Jacobs and Miss Feng jump as one.

"What are you kids doing back there?" snapped Deputy Jacobs, his brow furrowing.

"Oh, we were just watching your road detail," said Kate in a voice that told the deputy she wasn't to be messed with. "My brother and I didn't know there were Nazis working on the highway in Florida. Do people in town know about this?" asked Kate, hiking her thumb at the prisoners. "Boy, I don't think they'd be too happy to know how close these guys are to the beach! I wonder if anyone at the *Palm Beach Post* would like to hear about that."

The guard's mouth fell open. Miss Feng smiled a little. Charlie smiled back . . . and then he saw something out of the corner of his eye. It was only a flicker, but he was positive he'd seen it right:

One of the prisoners passed a small, folded piece of paper to another one. The two never looked away from Miss Feng, but their faces were set in concentration as they moved the paper from

hand to hand to pocket.

Charlie's skin prickled. They were hiding something. He didn't know how he knew, he just did.

He had to find a way to get that note. But how?

He shoved his hands in his pockets and felt something cool against his fingers. It all came to him suddenly. He felt a little disappointed—he *had* wanted ice cream—but this was too good to pass up.

"Oops!" said Charlie, unloading a handful of Mom's change on the ground. The coins hit the pavement and, just as he had hoped, went rolling on their sides toward the prisoners. Immediately, a handful of the POWs ran to pick up the coins—including the one who'd been passed the note, a mean-faced man with a sharp chin and a shock of yellow hair.

Charlie ran, bent at the waist, pretending to reach for one rolling quarter. He did a quick swerve, and—

BAM! Charlie and the prisoner crashed into each other. The man in the uniform staggered back, and then sneered at Charlie. "*Kleiner*

Schädling," muttered the POW, and seized Charlie by the collar. Charlie felt his heart beat fast as the Nazi lifted him, and smelled a blast of bad breath as he pulled Charlie's face close to his own—

Behind them, Charlie heard a rifle being cocked.

"Now, Reinhardt," said Deputy Jacobs calmly. "You'll be wanting to put that clumsy boy down. *Verständlich*?"

"Yes, boss," muttered the German between clenched teeth. He lowered Charlie to the ground, and Charlie trotted back to Kate, not even bothering to pick up his quarter.

"Are you okay, Charlie?" asked Miss Feng, looking surprised.

"Fine!" he said, grabbing Kate's arm as he passed them. "We'll see you around, Miss Feng. But I'll let our mom know we ran into you." He glanced at Deputy Jacobs. "You need our mom to send someone out here to walk you home? A Wave escort?"

"No, thank you, Charles," said Miss Feng, smiling as Deputy Jacobs looked away and grumbled. "I think you've done plenty already."

"Great," he said. "Come on, Kate."

Kate seemed to pick up on Charlie's anxiousness, and she didn't say anything until they were already a few hundred feet from the work detail. Finally, when they were closer to the town proper, she whispered, "What was that all about?"

"I'll tell you when we get home," he mumbled, reaching into his pocket and feeling the triangle of paper that he'd swiped from out of the German's uniform.

CHAPTER 10

JUNE 25, 1943
NORFOLK, VIRGINIA
8:54 A.M. LOCAL TIME

"And . . . go!"

Hank let go of Buster's collar, and Buster ran. He kept his eyes on the circle at the end of the course. That was his goal: the circle. Everything was the circle. He wouldn't let anything distract—

Ooh, sausage! Who left this big plate out here? Gross, it is cold. Look, Skipper is running. Oh man, I miss the sausage from home. Why'd they leave this out here? Maybe this was some kind of reward for—

He heard a snort in the distance. Remembered

the feeling of the horse's lips on the top of his head. Realized he was eyes-deep in the plate of sausage. Turned and sprinted.

By then, though, it was no use—Daisy and Skipper were already running up and over the little wooden hill in the middle of the obstacle course, and Freddy was squeezing through the tunnel carved through its center. Buster lowered his head and put all his energy into his legs, but by the time he was over the hill, the other two dogs were just smudges in the distance, and he was still behind.

Wait, where was Freddy? Buster heard a bark. Looked and saw a shadow moving in the tunnel. He got down on his front paws and saw Freddy struggling but stuck, maybe caught on something. Buster heard the panic in Freddy's bark as he tried to pull his way out but only wedged himself in farther.

Buster thought about the horse nibbling his head again, and a bit of sharpness—just a bit, not much but some—broke through the jumbled thoughts in his mind. Freddy needed help. Buster could do that. This wasn't any harder than digging up a crab on a beach.

Buster plunged his snout in the tunnel and gently mouthed around until he felt the tags on Freddy's collar. He bit, pulled, and *pop*, out came Freddy with a yip. The little dog looked up at Buster and danced back and forth for a moment before trundling on through the obstacle course. Buster turned and continued—

Ooh, a bowl of kibble! The kibble they have at this place is pretty lousy, but he'd eat it. He'd never turn down free food. Hey, there was Freddy. He'd helped Freddy! Felt bright today, huh? Brighter than usual. Hey, why'd they even put this kibble out if—

"Time," yelled Hank. He, Roy, and Nico walked out onto the obstacle course. Hank rubbed Buster's head and said, "Good boy, Buster," but Buster could hear the disappointment in his voice.

Oh no. Buster had done it again. He'd gotten distracted. He hadn't even reached the circle.

The three humans talked. They said a lot of the words they said around Buster all the time lately. *Bray-ver-ee. Con-sen-tray-shun.* Nico pointed at Buster a lot and spoke quietly but steadily. Roy shook his head. Hank spoke and said Freddy's name a lot. He pointed at the tunnel. They talked louder and louder, until Nico barked human words and the other two went silent.

After a moment, Hank came over to Buster. The human locked a leash on his collar, and said, "Buster" and "friends." The word made Buster brighten up a little, but Hank's voice was still pretty sad.

Hank led him around the back of the big buildings and out to the horse corral. Buster smelled his new friend—the big horse, the one the humans called *Anvil*—before he even saw him, and he launched himself forward so hard that Hank made a "WHUP!" noise and let go of the leash.

Sure enough, as Buster rounded the building, Anvil clopped over to greet him. One or two of the other horses behind the fence danced away a little as Buster came speeding toward them—the other dogs had scared them in the past—but Anvil didn't budge. He nodded his big thick head up and down and stomped his shaggy hooves as Buster arrived.

Buster ran circles around Anvil in his

excitement. He barked and barked, wondering if Anvil could understand him. He'd been in an obstacle course! There'd been sausage! He'd gotten distracted! He was a failure! Freddy got stuck, but Buster saved him! The kibble here isn't very good! It had been Anvil snorting when Buster had run the course, hadn't it? Buster had known! It had helped him—thinking of Anvil, remembering the head nibble! Knowing that Buster had a friend here, someone he could trust. It made him feel brave, like he had when Dad was still here.

Finally, he skidded to a halt beneath Anvil's nose. The big horse lowered his head and gave Buster a little scratch with his lips. Buster felt all the worry and confusion in him even out until he was just a dog alone with his thoughts. Two of the other horses came around and gave him a snort or a side-eye, but he remained in his calm place, the place where Dad had sent him with a scratch, where he'd gone when he'd heard the boy yell for help, where he'd gone halfway when Freddy got stuck.

A place Buster wished he could find on his own. A place of purpose.

After a few more lip-nibbles, Anvil stopped and neighed. Buster felt himself settle back into his normal mind, only maybe with a little less noise than usual. He looked up and gave Anvil a quick lick on the noise, which made the big animal whinny and shake his head, but not in an angry way . . .

There was a loud, low bark behind them. Anvil started back.

Buster turned to see Skipper standing at attention behind them, glaring at them. The soldier dog stared from Buster to Anvil and back again, her face set, her eyes hard. Finally, she settled her gaze on Buster. Slowly, she stepped forward, and as she did, Anvil and the other horses took a step back—not because they were worried she'd hurt them, Buster knew, but because of the air she gave off. Everything about Skipper was official, like a soldier. Buster would've backed away too, if her eyes hadn't pinned him to the spot.

Skipper stared Buster up and down. She turned her head, motioned back toward where Hank stood. The message was clear: get back where dogs belong. Buster whined—he wanted to spend more time with the horses. . . .

Skipper barked again, a little louder. The sound made Buster flinch, and he ran back over to Hank. As he and Hank left, Anvil snorted one final time, as though to remind Buster of the sound.

On his way back through the kennel room, Skipper followed, her hard gaze never leaving Buster. But as he passed them, Buster thought he saw Daisy and Freddy watching him. Their eyes were soft and grateful, as though they were happy he was here.

CHAPTER 11

JUNE 26, 1943
PALM BEACH, FLORIDA
1:14 P.M. LOCAL TIME

Charlie peered at the paper with the magnifying glass. Like that would help. Kate sighed at his stubbornness. Then she spun it around again. Like that was much better. She couldn't help it. She was frustrated.

"Anything?" she asked, hoping Charlie had made a breakthrough.

"Nothing." He sighed.

It was their third afternoon in a row sitting at the kitchen table, trying to figure out what the note said. The message was written in code—and it seemed like a pretty good one, Kate thought, though she admittedly had little experience with secret military codes. There were no words, just four or five letters and numbers at a time, clumped together, sometimes with an equals sign between them. They were written with a careful hand in dark pencil, so that they were unmistakable. But try as they might, she and Charlie couldn't make a lick of sense out of them.

"I still think the first word is 'dear,'" she said, pointing to the top of the page.

"Yeah, but why would a German prisoner send another German prisoner a letter?" asked Charlie.

Kate couldn't argue with that. She was grasping for straws. But it wasn't like she had any other choice. After all, she was eleven and had never left Florida. She'd heard on the radio news that the government needed huge, powerful machines to decipher coded German messages.

She pushed herself, the way Mom had taught her when she said she was going to give up math last year. What *would* the Germans be saying to each other? Obviously, it couldn't be something very good if they were hiding it from the guards (she doubted they were throwing Deputy Jacobs a surprise party). Plans for a revolt? Some sort of bomb-making recipe, maybe a blueprint of the prison they could use to stage a jailbreak? Or was it something simpler and sadder—a letter from home? News of a dead relative in the war?

She had another itch to call the cops, but then she quickly told herself to clam it. With the way those prisoners and their guards had joked with each other, she couldn't trust the grown-ups on this one. Besides, Dad always said, *If you want something done right, you have to do it yourself.*

She sighed. If only Dad were here. He'd be able to help for sure—Dad had always been so good at puzzles and games. He never read books or newspapers when they went out to the beach, but he filled out those big books of crossword puzzles he ordered in the mail. He always laughed about them with . . .

Bam!—just like that, it came to her.

"Mr. Hornby," said Kate.

"Who?" asked Charlie, and then his eyes lit up. "Oh shoot, you're right! The crosswords! Hold on." Charlie grabbed the paper and ran off into the apartment. Kate had barely hopped off her chair when Charlie came back with a brown leather folder under his arm.

Kate felt sparks go off beneath her skin.

"What are you doing?" she asked. Maybe a little too quickly, but still.

"What?" he asked. He followed her eyes, and held up the folder. "Oh, Dad's dossier. I thought since this is official business, like the binocs, we can—"

"*Careful*," she said. She snatched it out of his hand. Look at him, just waving it around. Did he think this was replaceable?

"Yeesh!" said Charlie. "Why can't *I* hold Dad's things once in a while?"

"Because you're so clumsy with them!" she said, clutching the dossier to her chest. "This isn't something you can just glue back together, Charlie. This belonged to Dad. We don't get his things back if they break or get messed up. That's how you lose the things that are most important to you—you act like a dummy with them."

Charlie huffed. "I'm the one who stole the note," he grumbled, and stomped off toward the door. Kate followed him quickly. She felt self-conscious but firm. Charlie liked to just barrel through things. Fall on the ground, run in the surf, scrape both knees at once. He was like Buster that way. She wouldn't let him guilt-trip her for wanting to protect what little of Dad she had left.

They went down to the courtyard, where Mr. Hornby sat in his canvas chair next to the victory garden. He wore a wide-brimmed straw hat, and, sure enough, he was doing a crossword in a big paperback book of puzzles. When he saw the twins coming toward him, he smiled and waved.

"Good morning, young friends," said Mr. Hornby. There was that weird accent again.

"Hi, Mr. Hornby," said Charlie. "Listen, we have a favor. We know you do puzzles a lot—have you ever tried to crack a code?"

Kate saw the emotion come over the man in one swoop, like a cloud's shadow on the ground.

Fear.

"Why d'ya ask, Charlie?" he said, closing his crossword book and lowering it into his lap.

"We found this note," said Kate, pulling the

paper from Dad's dossier and holding it out to Mr. Hornby.

The old man took the note in his wrinkled fingers and brought it close to his face. As his eyes moved across the page, Kate watched his mouth tighten and his nostrils flare. He was quiet for a long time.

"Mr. Hornby?" she asked.

"Horowitz," he mumbled.

A chill hit Kate. Mr. Hornby's accent had changed. Before, it was just strange. Now, it was thick . . . and definitely European.

"Sorry?" asked Kate.

"My name . . . is Marek Horowitz." The man sighed, eyes never leaving the page. "Where did you find the Ultra?"

"Sorry?"

"The *code*," he said, finally looking up at them. "Where did you find it? Who had it?"

"Why?" asked Kate.

"Because this is a Nazi code, children," said the old man, tapping the sheet with his index finger. "And the first word I recognize here is 'attack.'"

CHAPTER 12

JUNE 26, 1943
NORFOLK, VIRGINIA
1:18 P.M. LOCAL TIME

They all were walking back to the kennel—dogs and handlers, in a neat line. But Buster felt like every step he took was out of line. It'd been another rough day at the obstacle course, with Skipper refusing to even look at him. He just couldn't get it right.

He heard the neighing. His heart finally lightened. He lifted his head up and looked toward the sound.

Anvil? Yes, but not just Anvil—several horses! Lots of hooves, moving back and forth, up and down. What could it be? Buster wanted to find out.

He bolted, knowing that if he yanked as hard as he could, Hank couldn't hold on. Sure enough, the leash went flying out of Hank's hand, and Buster galloped across the property with it trailing behind him like a second tail.

When he came to the corral, what he saw filled him with a burst of excitement.

The horses had an obstacle course too! Some of them were jumping over white sections of fence. Others were dragging heavy black pieces of rock and metal that they pulled with their teeth or around their necks. There was even a tiny bridge over a ditch, like the one the dogs walked over (and Freddy went under), and a bunch of hoops that the horses had to lower their heads to walk through. All the while, Nico and one or two of the other humans led them along, whistling and lightly smacking them on the hindquarters with long, thin sticks.

Buster barked excitedly. He didn't know the horses had their own obstacle course! Why hadn't Anvil told him? He wanted to try it! He got along better with the horses than the other dogs, anyway. And this looked like fun! There was so much more jumping!

Before Buster knew it, he was under the fence of the corral and out among the horses. He felt energy surge through him as he ran, jumped—and cleared the section of fence! He sprinted over the bridge, running between another horse's legs and making her whinny and stamp. Then he was through the hoops! Then he dragged one of the big rocks across the lawn, using his teeth to pull the rope! Everything was noise and excitement and tension in his muscles! He was doing it! He was good at it! See?

He saw Anvil and ran over to him, barking and wagging his tail, his mind a blur, overjoyed, excited to show his friend everything he'd just done! Had Anvil seen? Everything was great! Everything was—

The big horse gave Buster a scratch on the head with his lips. Buster's mind calmed, and the cloud of excitement cleared away from his mind.

Everything, he quickly saw, was *not* great.

The obstacle course was clear. Some of the

horses were dancing around, spooked by Buster's barking and running; several of the humans were trying to calm them down. All of the humans—both those running the course and Hank at the fence—looked angry at Buster. Nico was marching over to him, fast.

Buster felt terrible. He'd just wanted to have fun with his horse friends. He didn't mean to cause any trouble! He just—

"Bad dog," snapped Nico. He swung his foot forward, and the toe of his boot dug into Buster's ribs.

Buster yelped and ran again. He knew he'd gotten in trouble for running off just now, but he was upset. His side hurt from Nico's kick, but his heart hurt from everyone's angry faces and the horses' loud neighs. He hadn't meant to mess everything up. He'd just gotten distracted.

He eventually stopped and caught his breath around the edge of the supply building. He sat with his side to the wall and wondered how he could be such a mess. Back at home, with Charlie and Kate, he was never a problem . . . or was he? The more he thought about it, the more memories rushed into his mind. Charlie shoving him away. Katie yelling and pushing him off of her. Mom crying when she found him lying by Dad's chair.

Had he *always* been a bad dog?

The idea made Buster whine out loud. Maybe he didn't belong here, or in Florida, or anywhere. Maybe he should just go away forever.

He finally got up and walked back toward the corral . . . and then he smelled something. Food.

His nose pulled him around the building, to an open door in the back. It dragged him inside, down a hall, and to the open door of a closet. And inside the closet was . . .

Buster froze.

Kibble. Three huge sacks of the dog food the humans gave them here. One of them open, leaning to the side. The perfect height for a muzzle to poke into.

Buster took a step toward the open bag. His stomach growled, and he had to lick his chops to keep from drooling. He wanted to eat it all. He was already a bad dog—maybe he should just go for it. He could barely hear the voice in the back of his head telling him that this would be it, the thing that got him sent away. Maybe that was okay, even if it meant making Hank sad, never seeing Anvil again or getting a nibble on the head—

He remembered the last nibble Anvil gave him and seemed to feel it again. Just like that, his mind cleared.

No.

He wouldn't eat the kibble. He would be a good dog. If he could do this—remember the scratch on his head, clear his mind without any help—then maybe he didn't have to be the bad dog everyone thought he was. He could be a soldier.

He turned away from the kibble, toward the door . . . and froze.

Skipper stood in the doorway, watching him.

Buster whined. He hadn't eaten the kibble. Did she see? He'd . . . he'd been a good dog . . .

Skipper started barking, loud. Buster heard footsteps approaching.

This wouldn't look good.

CHAPTER 13

JUNE 26, 1943
PALM BEACH, FLORIDA
1:50 P.M. LOCAL TIME

To Charlie, Mr. Hornby had been the ultimate sweet old man. Round at the waist, funny accent, did crosswords, liked to garden. Dad's good-natured conversations with the old man when he would take the twins to school or the park had been, in Charlie's mind, charity. Here was Dad, a big, strong sailor, talking to the lonely neighbor who lived in their building.

Marek Horowitz, the man who sat in front of him at his desk, was not that person. This man was sharp and serious, like Dad's old straight razor. This small, glowering man seemed to crackle with silent electricity, and spoke with a hard, sure voice that Charlie had never heard before today. His apartment was modern, but shadowy and cluttered with papers. His desk was new and made of cheap wood and plastic, but the milky photos around it were old, featuring dark-haired people in fancy clothing.

"You're lucky it's relatively simple," mumbled Mr. Horowitz, pointing his desk lamp at the paper. He ran a pencil beneath the jumbled numbers and letters on the page, and then scribbled other characters on a piece of scrap paper. Charlie watched as the man began to write words—not in English, but definitely words nonetheless.

"How did you know it was a Nazi code?" asked Charlie.

"Because that's what I did before I fled Czechoslovakia," said Mr. Horowitz. "I worked for the Czech government. I helped them decipher these sorts of codes . . . and came up with a few of my own." He narrowed his eyes at one of the words. "*Zellenblock*. That means cell block. Did this come from a prison?"

Charlie and Kate glanced at each other. Could they trust Mr. Horowitz? He could be some Czech code-breaker, like he claimed . . . or he could be a German spy. He'd known the code quickly enough, and he'd been living under a fake name. It was suspicious to say the least.

Kate shook her head ever so slightly.

"We found it in a bottle on the beach," said Charlie.

Mr. Horowitz paused and shot Charlie a dirty look, as though to say, *I'm not a moron, kid.* Then he turned back to the code. "It seems like a very important message to be floating around in a bottle . . ."

"Right?" Charlie chuckled. Kate frowned, and he couldn't blame her. It sounded unconvincing even to him. He looked for something else to talk about, and his eyes settled on the old photos around Mr. Horowitz's desk. "You have a . . . very nice family, Mr. Hornb—Mr. Horowitz. I hope they get a chance to visit soon."

Mr. Horowitz shook his head. "Not likely. My sister's family was taken to the camps."

"Camps?" asked Charlie.

Mr. Horowitz glanced up at him. "You don't know?" he said softly.

"Know what?" asked Kate.

Mr. Horowitz sighed and shook his head again. "Another time," he said in a hoarse voice. He wrote out a couple of words and lifted the scrap paper. "*Gehen Sie zum Nordrand . . . Head for the north side of the beach. Approximately 26.8 by -80.1. The . . . operatives will arrive ten p.m. Tuesday. Blackout, few civilians. Remain unseen. There will be a hole in the fence one hundred yards up. Operatives will come in uniform. Clothes, identification, and explosives waiting for you by purple . . . flag,* I believe, is the word, though it could mean other things. Then, it says to contact guard at cellblock B, who will have . . . *means to cut off the rail lines. To keep supplies and soldiers from leaving the state.*"

Charlie couldn't believe it. He'd heard about something like this before—Operation Pastorius, a plan to have German soldiers sabotage power centers and supply routes in New York. Nazi soldiers had come on shore in Florida and New York and had almost succeeded in their sabotage mission. Dad had read from the paper about it,

reminding them how crafty the Nazis could be.

Suddenly, he realized Mr. Horowitz was staring at him. Charlie's worries must've been painted all over his face, because the old man arched an eyebrow in disbelief. "So. Message in a bottle, eh, kid?"

"Yeah," stammered Kate. "We . . . found it while looking for shells on the beach."

"Well," said Mr. Horowitz, picking up the letter, "I suppose I should give this to the authorities, huh? The police will want to know—"

An image of Deputy Jacobs's smile flashed across Charlie's mind, and he yelped, "No!" In an instant, his hand snapped out and reached for the note from the prisoner and Mr. Horowitz's translation. "No, sorry, just . . . we'll take them! Our mother's in the Waves, so she can give them to the proper authorities. Sorry to bother you."

Mr. Horowitz placed his hand on the notes. "Why don't I hold onto these for now?"

"They're ours," said Kate sternly.

Mr. Horowitz arched an eyebrow at her . . . and then handed her the translation he'd made. "You can have the message," he said. "I'll keep the

Ultra. If you need it, you send your mother to me. And I'll tell you this, young Rankins—what matters is that whoever was *supposed* to get that note did not. Now, that said, it's Saturday. Tuesday is coming quickly. So be careful. For now, do me a favor. Give that to your mother. Keep a lookout for anything suspicious. And even if the guards, or the police, or anyone around you tries to tell you that the Germans really aren't that bad . . . don't believe them."

"We won't," said Charlie, and he rushed out of the small, dark apartment as quickly as he could.

Once they were outside, Kate didn't waste any time. "What do we do now?"

Charlie chewed the inside of his cheek and thought.

"We need to find a purple flag," he said. "And more important, we can't do this alone. Come on."

CHAPTER 14

JUNE 27, 1943
NORFOLK, VIRGINIA
2:03 A.M. LOCAL TIME

The smell and the word came together in his sleep at the same time and formed a single idea.

FIRE.

Buster sat up, and all at once he heard it, smelled it, felt it all around him. He barked, and one by one the other dogs in their kennels around him sleepily opened their eyes . . . and all stood and barked as well.

Fire. Flames. Danger.

Daisy and Freddy danced around the front

gates of their kennels and barked for the humans, barked to be let out and saved. But Buster knew better. He'd seen it around Palm Beach, whenever something dangerous happened around town, car crashes and fires and humans getting pulled out into the sea. If the humans were dealing with an emergency, they wouldn't think of the dogs. They'd be trying to help each other and stop the fire. He couldn't fault them for that; it's what they were supposed to do.

But the dogs were on their own.

Buster paced quickly, smelling the awful smoke from outside. Should he try to escape? Yesterday had been bad for him—when they'd found him in the kibble room, they'd assumed the worst. There'd been lots of yelling and *Bad dog, Buster!* and even a rolled-up magazine to his nose. He didn't want to get in any *more* trouble, and he knew that breaking out of his kennel was definitely a bad dog thing to do, even if there was a fire . . .

Somewhere, distantly, he heard a snort. Buster caught of a whiff of something burning—something specific. Hay.

The stable.

Oh no!

Buster felt a low growl build in his throat. They could call him bad dog all they wanted. Let Nico kick him in the side as many times as he felt like. Buster was going to make sure his friends were okay, bad dog or no.

He thought of Anvil's light nibble, and the top of his head buzzed. His mind focused. He backed up, ran forward, and threw himself against the front gate of his kennel. *BAM.* The grate held . . . but it bent. He did it again—*BAM.* It bent farther. The other dogs stared at him in awe. One more time—*BAM!*—and the grate swung outward. He was free!

Buster had to act fast. A flashing memory of the previous day's obstacle course came to him, and he ran to Skipper's kennel and nuzzled up the latch, barking for the other dogs to watch. He nosed up the little hook that latched her kennel shut, and just as it was almost out, Skipper threw herself against the grate—and it popped open. After Buster got Skipper out, he helped Freddy while Skipper helped Daisy.

The minute Freddy was free, Buster sprinted out into the night.

What he saw made the fur on the back of his neck stand up.

Three buildings were on fire—the soldiers' sleeping quarters were burning at one end, one of the big storage buildings was going up all over, and the stable had huge flames blazing out of a portion of the roof. Inside, the horses were whinnying and stamping their feet. Through all the noise, Buster could hear Anvil snorting and crying out. Sure enough, the humans were running around, trying to get water and put out the flames on the storage building and the soldiers' sleeping area. The stable could come later.

It was up to the dogs.

Buster ran to the stable door, where heavy loops of rope hung as handles. He jumped up and took one of the ropes in his mouth. It'd be just like pulling Freddy out of the tunnel in the obstacle course, he told himself . . . only a lot bigger.

As the sounds of the horses panicking filled his ears, he dug his back paws into the dirt, closed his eyes, and pulled, and *pulled* . . . but it was no use. The door was too heavy. It was stuck.

He tried again, listening to the cries of his friends, knowing that if they were hurt, it was because he had let them down. But he couldn't do it, he couldn't do any of it, he couldn't finish the obstacle course, he couldn't stop Dad from going away, he couldn't, he *couldn't*—

He felt another muzzle bite down on the rope.

Buster's eyes opened, and he saw Skipper next to him, growling softly as she pulled with him. The soldier dog shot him a look and let him know instantly: she was going to help him. Buster was right: it was up to them to save the horses.

Buster gave a muffled bark through the rope, and he and Skipper pulled at the same time, putting everything they had into it . . .

Snap—whatever was holding the door shut broke, and it swung open, letting out a blast of heat and smoke. Flames flowed across the ceiling of the stable like upside-down water, and embers rained everywhere, landing in the hay and creating tiny blazes of their own.

Buster and Skipper darted into the stable, and smoke burned their eyes and noses. Skipper barked and hunched low, getting beneath the stinging cloud. Buster realized what she was doing and imitated her.

They crept to the stalls where the horses stood. They hopped up on their hind legs and one by one nosed up the hooks latching the stable doors. The stalls flew open, and the horses galloped out into the night. Anvil was last and gave Buster a quick whinny before heading for the door. Buster went to follow him—

CRASH!

Buster started. He looked up to see a section of the roof on the floor of the stable, alive with fire. Skipper lay beneath it, her back legs pinned. She struggled to paw her way out, but she wasn't making any progress. Buster ran and tried to drag Skipper out by her collar, the way he'd pulled Freddy out of the tunnel—but the debris was too heavy.

Skipper whimpered.

He couldn't save her.

CHAPTER 15

JUNE 27, 1943
PALM BEACH, FLORIDA
4:46 P.M. LOCAL TIME

"This way," said Jeffrey, waving them toward the playhouse in his backyard. Kate thought the shack looked appropriate for a secret meeting—a little crumbly and ramshackle, a treehouse that had no tree to rest in. There was a heavy gray tarp instead of a door, and Jeffrey swept it aside officiously when they arrived, ushering Kate and Charlie into the shadowy space.

Kate had to stop herself from whistling, she was so impressed. They were all here—all the heavyweight neighborhood kids from military backgrounds, whose dads were overseas (*or*, she thought bitterly, *gone forever*) and most of whose moms were in the Waves or the SPARs, the coast guard's female reserves. The whole crew sat on benches around the playhouse or leaned against the flimsy walls. There was Jenny Turman, track star, tall and fast as a whip; Mickey Schultz, the gangly motormouth with all the best jokes; Chris Quintel, the towering bully with an angry brow; Maria Pantano, small and dark-haired, famous for sneaking into places better than any spy; Siobhan McLerner and her round-headed little brother, Will, their hair blazing red and their eyes bruised black from constant fights; Linda Brasser, quiet but pretty, smart as a rocket scientist, stricken with an awful crush on Charlie; and Joey Yamamoto, who could hit a baseball so hard it would fly all the way to Mexico.

Kate did a quick count—with them and Jeffrey, they had eleven. She thought that would be enough, but she knew the going was about to get tough.

"Hi, guys," said Kate, raising a hand. "As Jeffrey's probably told you, we called you here because we've got a problem. We think there might be a secret plan for Nazi soldiers to infiltrate Palm Beach. And we need to stop them."

The gathered crew murmured and shot each other suspicious looks. As usual, Mickey Schultz spoke first.

"Aw, come on, Rankin," he said. "That's some pretty silly stuff. I know you two like watching for U-boats down by the beach, but that don't mean there's some secret plot going down."

"Actually, we have proof," said Charlie. "I don't know if you guys know this, but there's a crew of POWs from Tampa working on the roads outside of town."

The other kids murmured again, but Maria Pantano nodded. "Along Route One," she said. "Fixing the fence."

"Right," said Kate. "The other day, we intercepted a message from one of them."

"Was that when Charlie did that thing by spilling the change from his pockets?" asked Maria. Kate stared at her in surprise, and Maria shrugged. "You two aren't very hard to follow."

"In any event," said Charlie, "we had it

translated, and it had coordinates . . . well, listen." He pulled the folded-up note from his pocket and read the message out loud. The kids all glanced at one another, some in horror, others less convinced.

"Kinda flimsy proof, twerps," growled Chris Quintel.

"I believe you, Charlie," said Linda softly.

"So, okay, let's say this checks out," said Mickey. "Why exactly are we talking about it? Why not just tell the cops, or our moms or whoever? We're just kids."

"The guards we saw were pretty friendly with the prisoners," said Charlie. "We're worried the cops might only listen to them, not us."

"And all our moms are barely around, what with helping the war effort," said Kate. "Besides, you know grown-ups. They focus on all the wrong things, and they talk too much. Nobody gets anything done."

The gathered crew nodded and mumbled agreement. Every one of them knew firsthand just how ineffective adults were when it came to actually doing anything.

"So, what do we do?" asked Mickey. "Let's say we find this purple flag—so what? Are we supposed to be out there so late at night, and during a blackout? My pop'll kill me."

"What if we put a bunch of purple flags on the beach?" asked Will Lerner. "That way, they won't know which one has their supplies under it."

"Will, let someone smart talk," said Siobhan, rolling her eyes.

"Shut up, Siobhan," he said, shoving her.

"You shut up," she said, shoving him back.

"Fight!" yelled Mickey. A couple of the other kids echoed his excitement. Kate watched as they all started getting distracted, talking among themselves, forgetting why they were here. She felt panic and anger rising in herself, thinking there was nothing she could to do wrangle them back in—

"The Germans killed our dad!"

All conversation stopped at once, and all eyes, including Kate's, turned to Charlie. Her brother stood there frozen, his glazed eyes staring off into space, his hands clutched at his sides.

"He was on a submarine outside of Honduras,

and a U-boat shot it with a torpedo," said Charlie. He swallowed hard, and a big fat tear plunked down his cheek. "They didn't even find him. We just got a letter."

Kate gasped. She couldn't believe he'd said that out loud. Tears flooded her eyes, and her throat ached. Silence fell over the playhouse.

"My pops got shot down over the Atlantic," murmured Jenny Turman.

"Mine's in a hospital in England," said Chris. "Telegram said he lost an arm."

One after another, all of the kids began naming places they'd never been, regiments, branches of the military. All of them knew about the war, even if they'd never left Palm Beach.

"We all have family out there, right now," said Charlie in a hoarse voice. "Whether they're fighting in Europe, or the Pacific, or here at home, they're risking their lives for us. For our country, for America. Well, I'm not going to let the people who killed my dad . . . who want to see us all dead or conquered . . . I will *not* let them come here and attack our home from the inside out. So Kate and Jeffrey and I, we're doing our part. We'll be out there, protecting our home. If you're in, let us know. And if not . . . well, there's the door."

"It's more of a tarp," said Mickey. Chris leaned over and swatted him on the back of the head.

"Whatcha got in mind, Charlie?" asked Siobhan.

Charlie turned and smiled at Kate. "Kate's always been the smart one in the family," he said. "I'll let her explain the plan."

Kate smiled at her brother. She wanted to hug him but figured that could wait. There was work to be done.

"Okay," she said, turning back to the crowd and relishing how they all leaned in. "Here's what I'm thinking. First, we've got to make sure we're right about the code . . ."

CHAPTER 16

JUNE 27, 1943
NORFOLK, VIRGINIA
2:32 A.M. LOCAL TIME

Fire raged all around Buster as he leaped back and forth. Skipper still struggled to get out from under the chunk of roof, her claws scraping against the floor . . . but it was no use. She was stuck, and the fire was getting worse and worse.

Buster barked in panic. What could he do? He'd been a good dog . . . but he couldn't fix this!

Then he heard a snort and looked up—Anvil was at his side. The horse lowered his head and used his huge snout to lift the piece of debris ever so slightly. Buster pulled, Skipper clawed, and finally, she crawled out from under the heavy hunk of wood. Then the two dogs and the horse turned and sprinted out into the cool night air. Right as they got out of the stable, there was a sharp crack, and the rest of the roof caved in with a deafening blast of noise and heat.

By now, the humans had caught up with them. Some were corralling the dogs and horses who had left the stable, while others were using great big spray cans to put out some of the flames. Hank, wearing his pajamas, looked up to see Buster trotting toward him, and a funny little smile formed on his face. Buster wagged his tail at the sight of it . . . and only then realized that for the first time in a while, he hadn't gotten distracted. He'd been clear-headed for the whole adventure.

Hank dropped to one knee and wrapped his arms around Buster's neck, the way Charlie had the day Buster left Florida.

"Good boy," he whispered. "Good boy, Buster."

Buster stared over Hank's shoulder at Skipper. The war dog stood perfectly still in the light from the fire and didn't make a sound. But then, slowly, she walked over to Buster . . . and gave him a lick.

Buster wondered what they were talking about behind that door. The floor he was on was cold. He could smell a peanut under that bench. Outside, a raccoon was in the garbage again. Why was he in here, sitting in this dark, metal-floored room in the soldiers' meeting place? He hoped he wasn't in trouble.

He could hear muffled bits in the crack underneath—mainly his name, and the names of some of the other dogs, but a few other words he'd heard a lot lately that he'd begun to understand a little. *Brave* and *obstacle course*, for starters. *Coo-ord-in-nay-shun* was another one. So was *mi-shun*. That one was being used a lot. They also kept mentioning somebody named *Hor-o-witz*, and talking about his *in-tell*. That was important to the *mi-shun*.

And then there were two phrases he understood, but he didn't know why they were being said: *ready* and *not ready*.

What could they be talking about?

He huffed. This was another strange moment. Things had been a blur since the fire, and not just because the humans had to move a lot of boxes and stable some of the horses in the storage building. All day, Hank had kept asking him to show Roy and Nico how he opened the stable door using the rope. Whenever Buster showed him, Hank would point at him and say, "THAT!" and then would yell a bunch of human words. Buster wasn't sure what that meant—was he doing a good thing? A bad thing? He was trying! He'd saved Anvil and the other horses! Wasn't that enough?

On top of that, the other dogs were being weird around him . . . but not in the same way as before. Before, it had been obvious—they were war dogs, well trained and good at their jobs, and he was bad. Now, they all treated him like . . . well, Buster didn't know! Like Buster was some sort of special dog, who they didn't understand. They'd done the obstacle course again, and twice Daisy and Freddy stopped and just watched what Buster was doing. Skipper, meanwhile, was being helpful but physical. She'd nudge him away from the kibble, or leap over the wooden boxes and then run back around and do it with him. What was going on?

He tried to think more, but it hurt his head. He'd been so focused lately, but it was still hard to keep up. His ear itched. The raccoon had found an apple core. Out in the field, one of the horses was eating a carrot. Did Skipper think he was stupid? Hank raised his voice in the room. What were they talking about in there?

The door opened. Nico was the first to come out, and he pointed at Buster and said a word Buster knew down in his bones: "NO." Buster sat up, scared. "NO" usually meant he'd done something bad. What could it be? He hadn't even eaten that peanut under the bench!

Hank sighed. Tossed up his hands. Came over, snapped a leash on Buster's collar, and walked him away. Buster whined and hunched his shoulders. Whatever he'd done, it must've been pretty bad.

Hank took him out of the building . . . and away from the pens, toward the cars. Buster's heart sank, and he whimpered louder. The last time he'd been in a car, it was to take him away from Charlie and Kate. That's what this must be. He was being asked to leave, for whatever he'd done. Maybe he hadn't been supposed to save the horses. Well, that was silly, and he was glad he had. They were his friends.

"Sorry, Buster." Hank sighed. He said some more human words, and then said the word Buster was expecting: "Goodbye."

Buster glanced around at the sunny countryside. He guessed this was it. It was over—

A wind. A flash of smell.

Skipper stood at his side. She didn't jump or bark. She just sat down next to him, gave him a quick smell, and looked up at Hank.

Buster heard footsteps behind him, and Nico and Roy came jogging up to meet Hank. Nico reached for Skipper's collar, but she pulled away from him. Nico stepped back and said, "Skipper, come," but Skipper gave a soft *whuff* and stayed still.

Buster realized what was happening. The ache in his heart was like a million head-scratches at once, making him feel smarter and stronger and *good dogger* than ever.

Hank looked at Nico. Said some human words about *Hor-o-witz. Mi-shun. Tomorrow.*

Buster woofed, and Skipper—his friend, his partner—woofed back.

He knew right then that he wasn't going anywhere. That his work here had just begun.

CHAPTER 17

JUNE 28, 1943
PALM BEACH, FLORIDA
9:40 P.M. LOCAL TIME

Charlie looked back at their town and goose bumps crept across his flesh. Everything was dark, a series of huge black shapes barely visible against the cloudy sky. The most he got was the occasional outline of a window, or a blink of light as someone peeked out from under their blinds before a block warden signaled for them to stop. Otherwise, the city was bathed in total darkness.

He'd never seen a blackout from outside their apartment—heck, he'd never even imagined it. Now, he was surprised at how well it worked.

Given how little light he could see from here, there was no way an enemy sub or plane could catch a glimmer from miles out.

"Charlie," whispered Kate, elbowing him. Charlie yanked his eyes off the skyline and tried to focus. Look at him, getting distracted when he was about to embark on a dangerous home front war mission. Who was he, Buster?

He and Kate kept low as they snuck toward the section of beach up by Wells Road that Linda Brasser had helped them identify as the coordinates on the map. In Kate's pocket, Charlie could see the thick round bulge of Linda's masterpiece—made from stuff Maria had swiped from the school science lab and her parents' hardware store. He reached into his own and felt the cold metal square of Dad's old Zippo lighter. They were ready.

Charlie couldn't believe they'd all made this happen in twenty-four hours. If their plan worked out . . .

They got almost to the top of a grass-covered sand dune and crouched down. Charlie thought he could see Joey next to another dune, but he wasn't sure. He gave the signal—three high-pitched whistles, doing his best to sound like a sandpiper—and heard them back.

The twins crept to the silhouette in the dark, and sure enough, it was Joey, carrying the Louisville Slugger he'd gotten two Christmases ago. When they were close enough, he spun the bat and whispered, "You get the bomb?"

"It's not a bomb," said Kate. "But yes. Everyone in position?"

"Chris is patrolling the streets up there, to stop anyone who might be coming our way," said Joey, nodding back toward the houses deeper on the inland side of the beach. The houses stood just far enough back to keep them out of view. "Mickey's up on a hill somewhere—if he sees anything, he's going to run around making noise until we get noticed. And if this works, he'll send up an alarm."

"He's good at that," said Charlie. "Any word from Siobhan and Will about the purple flags the prisoners are looking for?"

"None yet—"

"Hey." They all started and whirled around.

Jenny Turman stood next to them, looking rangy and sweaty. She put her hands on her knees and caught her breath.

"Siobhan and Will found the flag," she said, pointing a thumb over her shoulder. "About ten minutes or so ago, a mile away. Big bag of clothes and what look like blasting caps, buried in the sand under some purple paint on a post. They've taken everything out, and now they're posting up. They say they'll fight anyone who comes near it. Siobhan says she wants to punch a Nazi, like Captain America."

Charlie nodded, impressed. He knew Jenny could haul, but a mile in ten minutes was even faster than he had imagined. "Any word from Jeffrey?"

"Yeah, saw him earlier today," said Jenny. "He says he tried to contact his brother, but it's no use. He's out on a mission or something."

"Okay," said Kate. "Other than that, I think everyone's actually in place. This . . . this should work."

"Yup," said Jenny. She stood up and wiped her brow. "You have Linda's bomb?"

"It's not a bomb," said Charlie.

"Whatever, her firework," said Jenny.

"We have it," said Kate. She reached into her pocket and pulled out a thick round orb wrapped in a layers of tight canvas. It was a little bigger than a baseball, and had a small tail sticking out of the side. Charlie had to admit, in the darkness it looked like the bombs he'd seen in the cartoons when Dad had taken him to the movies. And according to Linda, it was full of charcoal, magnesium, and sulfur—all of which sounded like things that could blow up at a moment's notice.

Joey took the firework and gave it a toss in the air with one hand.

"Careful," said Kate. "We only get one shot at this."

"Linda's sure this won't break up when I hit it?" asked Joey. "It's not as hard as a baseball."

"This is Linda Brasser we're talking about," said Charlie. "She's top of our class and a chemistry whiz. If anyone's going to be right about these sorts of things, it's her. Just don't hit it too hard—we need to this to go high and far. But honestly, if it goes kind of slow, that's fine. The longer it's in the air, the more we can see . . . and the more they'll think they've been caught."

"High, far, slow," said Joey. "Got it. Do you have the lighter—"

"Hey, you!"

All of them turned at once. Charlie felt terror spike in his heart.

A young man in a short-sleeved shirt and white cap stormed up over the dune behind them—a coast guardsman, by the looks of him. He dragged Chris Quintel by the ear after him.

This . . . this could be a serious problem.

"What're you kids doing out during the blackout?" demanded the coast guardsman. He started to march down the beach and stumbled, his feet sliding in the sand.

Charlie saw their chance.

"Kate, you and Jenny go tell him what's going on," he said. "Joey, it's now or never."

Kate paused, looking unsure—and then ran toward the coast guardsman, waving her arms. "Sir!" she cried. "We've intercepted a secret message. There's a U-boat in that water, and it's sending German spies onshore!"

The coast guardsman froze, and a frown crossed his face. "Who told you that?"

Kate kept talking, but Charlie wasn't listening. He pulled the Zippo from his pocket and gave a few flicks of the wheel. Would it work? Was there enough lighter fluid? They hadn't used it since Dad died.

He flicked it hard . . . and lit a small flame. Joey held the flare out and touched the fuse to it. With a hiss, the fuse lit up in a bright sizzle. Behind them, the coast guardsman began to yell louder, but Charlie was so focused on lighting the flare, he couldn't make out what the man was saying.

"One shot," said Charlie breathlessly.

"Rankin, that's all I need," said Joey. He hefted the ball into the air, stepped back, raised his bat, and just as the ball began to fall—

WHAP! Joey hit the flare solidly. Charlie watched the fizzling ball soar high out over the ocean. Behind them, the conversation died as the group watched its flight.

Just before it reached its peak, the flare lit up with a blinding pink light and a nasty hiss. In the burning light it gave off, the whole beach and at least a half mile of ocean were perfectly illuminated.

Either the U-boat thinks it's been spotted and flees, thought Charlie, *or, with any luck, we see . . .*

Out in the water swayed a dinghy with paddles on either side. On it, four men in German uniforms stared up at the flare with wide eyes and open mouths.

Charlie gasped. He pointed, but the words couldn't come out.

"Jenkins!" screamed the coast guardsman back toward town. "Jenkins, get the radio! We're under attack!"

CHAPTER 18

JUNE 28, 1943
PALM BEACH, FLORIDA
9:15 P.M. LOCAL TIME

It hit Buster the minute they got off the plane.

Home. He was home.

His ears went up, and his nostrils flared. His head darted back and forth, agitated. *Home! Charlie and Kate and Mom! The beach! The ocean! Chasing the ball, licking Charlie's face! His spot by the chair—*

Stop. He imagined the scratch on his head, and the focus came to him bit by bit. He couldn't lose sight of what he needed to do. He knew it hadn't been that long since he'd left home, but for

Buster, that time had meant everything to him. If he was home and Skipper and Hank were here, it was because there was something they had to do.

Beside him, silent and ready, stood Skipper, her midsection wrapped in bandages. Buster watched her and sensed how strong she was, even after being wounded by the falling debris during the fire. Even though he could sense a faint whimper somewhere deep in her throat, he never saw her flinch as she faced off with the humans. She looked at him, and though it was no longer in the angry way she'd done before, he could tell that she wasn't here to play. He better be ready.

This, Buster understood, was the *mission.* Somewhere out there was the big scary thing he'd heard the humans talk about for so long. He was ready to meet the *war.*

Hank drove them toward the ocean for a while, and then he let them out near a stone dock, where a ship was waiting for them with a few other soldiers on it. Buster had seen boats like this from the shore all the time, patrolling the water. The men on them had white, diamond-shaped hats like the one Hank and Roy wore now. Sometimes

Charlie would wave to them, and the men would wave back.

Hank led him down a ramp and onto the top of the boat. "This is Buster," he said, and some of the soldiers rubbed Buster's face and his neck. Then Roy came on board and said, "Skipper," and everyone went crazy! Buster jumped as the humans clapped and took off their hats, and went to pet Skipper while saying, "Good girl!" and "Atta girl, Skipper!" Skipper, for her part, looked calm, if a little embarrassed.

Buster got it now: this wasn't Skipper's first fight. The shiny metal pieces on the wall of her kennel, her leg wound—she had done this plenty of times before.

The two dogs walked to the front of the boat, and Buster smelled the gasoline mixing with the sea air as the boat rumbled to life beneath his paws. Slowly, the ship turned out into the dark water, cutting through waves and sending foam flying up into Buster's face.

He thought about how not long ago, all of this would have made him feel crazy. And in a way, it still did—he smelled everything, heard

everything, and wanted to be a part of it. He wanted to leap around the boat and put his paws up on every soldier and dive over the edge at the fish he saw jumping as they passed.

But he wouldn't. That sharp stillness in his mind, that feeling like he knew exactly what needed to be done, was still there. And he intended to ride it as far as he could take it.

Hank came up behind him and rubbed his back. "Good boy, Buster," he said softly. "Doing great."

They headed out onto the dark, huge ocean. The moon was barely visible beneath a layer of clouds; other than that, it was total blackness. Buster listened to the humans around him talking, whispering about *intel* and *coordinates.* He looked out at the size of the sea and thought about how big it really was, how he'd never been this far out onto it. Where were they, even? He'd lost the smells of home; all he could pick up were the salt of the water, the gas of the ship, and Skipper next to him. He looked back to where the shore would be—but it was gone. There was just black.

He whined softly. Was this the *war?* Had the

monster swallowed them? Were they in the belly of the war, with no way out? He hoped not. He hoped he would get to see Charlie and Kate and Anvil and Freddy and Daisy again.

They drifted silently in the darkness for a while longer. Every so often, the boat turned and went in a different direction, but Buster didn't see anything but big walls of shadow. Maybe they were done for. The idea made him feel very scared, and he whined even louder, but Skipper turned and gave him a quick nuzzle and a lick to the face. She wanted him not to worry, and Buster decided that if Skipper wasn't scared, he wouldn't be either.

Slowly, the boat began to turn around, back the way it came.

HISS.

Buster jumped and looked to the sky. A ball of light was glowing off in the distance, like an extra-bright star, flickering so bright that it hurt Buster's eyes. In its light, he could see the shore, and people on it . . . and people on the water as well, in a smaller boat!

Wait.

Buster heard something else too. Something deeper and scarier.

He turned from the light and ran to the edge of the ship. He listened, and pushed his eyes as hard as he could, and . . .

There, out in the water.

He barked. He barked like crazy. Skipper came bounding over to him, looking concerned—and then she heard it, too, out in the water.

Just as the humans' radios came alive with screaming voices, a great shape moved under the water in the distance. It hummed deeply, turned around beneath the waves, and came gliding toward them.

CHAPTER 19

JUNE 28, 1943
PALM BEACH, FLORIDA
10:05 P.M. LOCAL TIME

Kate couldn't believe how fast everything happened.

One minute, the hapless coast guardsman was running off over the dunes, leaving Chris Quintel to rub his ear. Charlie's hand still hung in the air as he pointed out into the water where a raft full of Germans bobbed on the surface.

The next, total chaos broke loose.

A raid siren rang out from shore, low at first but then rising in volume and pitch like the angriest cat in the world. The Germans leaped off their boat one after another and swam toward shore for all they were worth. Just as Linda Brasser's magnesium flare hit the ocean and finally fizzled out, a bell clanged over the water.

Three coast guard Jeeps came blasting over the dunes and onto the beach, spraying sand everywhere. They skidded to a halt by the water's edge, and two of them lit up with huge spotlights affixed to their backs. They shone them out on the dark water, locating the swimming Nazis and following them as they got closer to the shore.

One of the coast guardsmen, a huge man with a broad face and a little white hat, jogged over to them.

"What are you kids doing here?" he bellowed. "This is officially a US Coast Guard operation! We need you to go back to your homes, NOW!"

"We're the ones that sent up the flare!" yelled Kate over the noise.

A stunned look of surprise crossed the officer's face—but he quickly shook his head, and his angry expression returned. "Well . . . good work, kids. Where'd you get a flare?"

"We built it," said Joey.

"You built—look, we just need you to get out of here," said the coast guardsman, peering at the kids as though they were the funniest-looking animals in the zoo. "Things are about to get really dangerous out there, and we can't have you getting hurt."

"Officer, do you know if a guardsman named Hank Collins is part of your team?" asked Kate, feeling a prickle of excitement in her chest. "Tall man, very handsome, usually works with dogs?"

"I don't know him," said the guardsman, throwing up his hands. "Look, *go home*, kids! We don't need you getting in trouble out here." He sighed. "But nice work. You did good."

"You got it, sir," said Kate—and gave Charlie a quick wink. "Come on, guys."

She waved the others back and began to head toward the street . . . until she saw over her shoulder that the coast guardsman had gotten far enough away. Then she turned and sat down just behind a dune. Without a word, Charlie, Joey, Jenny, and Chris all did the same. They didn't need to say anything, because they all knew what Kate was doing. They weren't going to miss this for the world.

One by one, the Germans got to the shore and rose from the surf with their uniforms heavy and soaking wet. The coast guardsmen were waiting for them with raised pistols and rifles, yelling for the Nazis to show their hands. The invaders stepped clumsily forward in the harsh light of the spotlights, their hands up and their faces frozen in resignation. The coast guardsmen grabbed them harshly and walked them to their vehicles.

As Charlie and Kate watched, the other kids from their team—Mickey, Jeffrey, the Lerner siblings—walked up and sat down next to them. Mickey gave Charlie a chuck on the shoulder, and Chris and Joey slapped five. Kate wondered if they should've made popcorn.

A sound came over the water. Loud, steady . . . barking.

Kate's ears and mouth dropped open.

Could it be?

She looked at Charlie, and she could tell he was thinking the same thing. He stared out at the water in disbelief, his hands planted in the sand to steady himself. Kate pulled Dad's binoculars

from her pocket and stared through them, trying to make out exact shapes on the dark water.

"Is there a dog out there?" asked Mickey.

On the water, a spotlight lit up. It panned across a midsized cutter ship, one of the coast guard's patrolling boats, about sixty feet long. Through the binoculars, Kate saw it illuminate the shapes of men standing on the deck . . . and two dogs that looked a lot like Labradors. Were her eyes playing tricks on her, or was it . . .

"Buster!" she cried. "It has to be!"

They all watched as multiple spotlights came alive on the cutter and moved along the water. The circles of light on the surface began to draw together, until they focused on an area about a quarter mile in the distance.

The sea bulged . . . and Kate saw the darting neck of a periscope.

She couldn't believe it. After all these weeks of watching from the shore. Of peering through the sweaty rings of Dad's binoculars. And it was actually . . .

"A U-boat," mumbled Charlie. He reached out and took Kate's hand, and without thinking she squeezed back.

Suddenly, the night was filled with noise and flashing light. The guns on the coast guard ship began firing into the spotlit section of the water, sending bursts of foam soaring high in the air. The clank of bullets hitting the U-boat's hull joined the noise of the night.

Without thinking, Kate and Charlie cheered. All of the other kids behind them did the same. Even the coast guardsmen down on the beach were yelling along, too, shouting for the ship to keep firing. "Take 'em down!" "Show no mercy!" Kate loved it.

Kate heard a groan of metal. A muffled thud, and a *whoosh*.

The water rippled, surging in a straight line toward the cutter.

Suddenly, the cheers turned to shouts and screams as everyone on shore watched what was happening.

"Torpedo!" shouted Kate so hard her throat hurt. "It's going to—it's—"

The ripple hit the coast guard ship, and—

BOOM!

Kate squinted as she felt the force of the blast against her face.

The night lit up with fire. Pieces of the cutter flew everywhere. Kate could see a few coast guardsmen splashing in the water . . . but there was no sign of the dogs.

Kate lowered her binoculars, dumbstruck. She and Charlie looked at each other, stunned.

"Just," muttered Charlie, "just like—"

Kate wouldn't let him finish the thought. They had to be strong, like Mom was, like all the soldiers who gave their lives for America had been.

She watched the coast guardsmen from the trucks rush toward the surf. "We need to help them," she said.

Charlie snapped his gaping mouth shut and nodded. "Human chain?"

"Let's do it," said Kate. She turned to the gathered kids behind her, face tight with determination. "Guys, those sailors need our help. You ready?"

"Let's do this!" shouted Mickey, and the kids leaped to their feet and sprinted toward the water.

CHAPTER 20

JUNE 28, 1943
PALM BEACH, FLORIDA
10:13 P.M. LOCAL TIME

For a moment, there was nothing.

The rush of wind through his fur. The smell of burning. All sound drowned out into a single loud *CRUNCH.*

Then, *crash,* and he was flying into the water.

Buster landed with a splash, and the force sucked him deep under the water.

He twisted beneath the waves, trying to understand where he was. The noises were muffled, the voices seemed to come from far away, and every few seconds something heavy would rush past him and sink farther and farther. In the distance, he could hear something huge moving and churning—maybe the *war*, he thought, finally swimming toward him, ready to eat him. He realized that for all the time he'd spent in water as a dog from Florida, he hadn't gone underwater very much, and suddenly he felt gripped by fear.

Buster focused. There—light, swimming shapes of men. He kicked his legs, and moved upward, upward, until *SPLASH*—his muzzle broke the surface.

The world above the water was just as scattered and crazed as the one below. Why was it so dark? He couldn't smell anything. Was he still *under* the water? He hadn't done that before! What was the big creature churning off in the distance—was that the *war?* Where had the boat gone? And Hank! And Skipper! And—

He could barely believe his eyes. How had all of this happened in a few seconds?

The boat floated around him in huge pieces and little bits. Somehow, there was fire on the surface of the water, lighting up the night in flickers and flashes. The only thing he could clearly

smell was the thick smoke coming off the fires. All of the soldiers from the boat were bobbing in the sea, shouting and trying to get ahold of larger hunks of the boat. Most of them were heading to shore, swimming as hard as they could, dragging other soldiers with them. He could hear voices all around, from the sea and the beach, calling "Come!" and "Here!"

Buster looked at the soldiers, looked around the pieces of boat on all sides of him.

No Hank.

Hank! Where was Hank? Buster needed to find him. Man, that smoke smelled bad. No, wait, he needed to keep his head clear. Hank should be yelling. He was a loud human. Buster barked and spun in the water, calling out to his friend, searching the surface with his eyes . . .

There.

Hank floated facedown in the ocean.

Buster's mind focused instantly.

He paddled so hard it hurt. He reached Hank in no time and used his muzzle to flip the human over. Hank's eyes blinked, but not at the same time. He tried to talk but wasn't able to. He looked to Buster like the sickest human he'd ever seen, worse than that time Kate had had to lie in bed for a week and the doctor had come over.

Buster grabbed Hank's sleeve between his teeth and pulled. He kicked and kicked, but the human was still heavy in the water, and he was too dazed to help swim. Pieces of the boat kept bumping into Buster, getting stuck under his chin or up against Hank's body. Buster couldn't get the human to move fast enough.

What a terrible dog he was. No help at all. Hank was going to be hurt, Hank was going to *die*, all because Buster was too weak to—

A bark. Buster look up to see a huge piece of the boat moving toward him . . . with Skipper on the other side, paddling it forward. Buster couldn't believe it!

He dragged Hank over to the hunk of boat—a piece about as big as two of the doors in Kate and Charlie's apartment, if not bigger—and shoved Hank's limp body against it. The feeling of the solid piece of wood and metal seemed to wake

Hank up a bit, because he rolled over in the water and threw his arms onto the piece of wreckage.

Buster swam over to the other side of the hunk of boat, put his paws up next to Skipper's, and paddled alongside her. At first, he didn't think they could do much to push a big piece of wood with a soldier draped on it, but pretty soon they were motoring along. He knew Skipper had the right idea—she was a smart dog and had obviously been in these kinds of situations before.

"HELP!"

Buster's head whipped so hard, he nearly yanked the piece of the debris out from under Skipper.

He listened closely. Splashing, shouting, screaming children. A voice.

Had he heard that right?

"HELP!"

Yes. There it was.

Buster barked loudly, telling the voice that he was coming, to hold on for one minute. He launched himself into the water and swam. Skipper barked loudly, angry at him for deserting her with Hank still in danger, but Buster couldn't really hear her.

He had to follow the voice. He had to find it, to save it.

Because the voice was Charlie's.

CHAPTER 21

JUNE 28, 1943
PALM BEACH, FLORIDA
10:29 P.M. LOCAL TIME

"Keep 'em coming!" cried the coast guardsmen, waving from where they stood waist-deep in the surf.

Charlie struggled against the currents of the cool water. He reached out, and the sailor swimming toward him grabbed his hand. He pulled the struggling man in, and the sailor grabbed onto Kate's shoulder. Then he moved to Mickey, and then to Jenny, Chris, and the other coast guardsmen who had joined their human chain. Charlie watched the sailor move down the line until he crawled, retching and gasping, onto the sand.

Charlie felt his arm ache as he put it out again, trying to feel for another body in the water. He'd lost count of how many men they'd grabbed and given passage back to shore. A cutter-class ship this big could have up to twenty or twenty-five men on it, but it seemed like even more. Some were swimming hard; others were injured or barely conscious. The coast guardsmen who'd joined them were doing a good job of taking on a lot of the strain. But out in the ocean, treading water, clinging to Kate's hand for dear life, Charlie was starting to feel exhausted.

All the while, he kept his eyes open for a dog. He could *swear* one was barking near him . . .

He scanned the surface, looking for other crew members from the cutter who could use his help. In the distance, flickering oil fires on top of the water and smoke from the wreck made it hard to see. Mostly, there was just debris floating around them, boards and metal rods bobbing in the waves. Maybe he'd gotten them all.

Charlie's eye caught a glimmer in the water—a

belt buckle, illuminated by the flaming oil in the distance. There was another man floating in the ocean about twenty feet from him. By the looks of it, he was almost drowned—his skin was so white that it seemed to glow in the dark water, and his uniform jacket had a smear of dark red on it. His body rose and fell with breath ever so faintly, telling Charlie he was still alive . . .

Charlie squinted. Wait, why would a patrolling coast guardsman have an officer's jacket on? And there was something else about the man—the color of his hair, the shape of his face . . . it was unfamiliar . . . it was . . .

The realization hit him with a chill that made the warm Florida surf feel like ice water.

It was one of the Germans from the raft.

Charlie felt his mouth go dry. Right there, in front of him, was one of the men whose people had killed his dad. One of the spies trying to infiltrate his country, to bring the war to his home.

If Charlie helped him, he might live to hurt more Americans. He might help organize another plot to infiltrate American soil.

If Charlie didn't, the man would die for sure.

"Kid!" called one of the coast guardsmen behind him. "Are there any more? Should we pull you in?"

"We still have to get the dogs!" Kate called out. "And it looks like there's one more person in the water." She tightened her grip on Charlie's arm. "Charlie, can you reach him?"

Charlie stretched out his arm as far as he could . . . but the German officer was too far away. His arm cried out in pain . . . but it just wasn't possible.

The man would die.

Maybe he deserved to.

But if you don't help him, thought Charlie, *how are you any better*?

Charlie let go of Kate's hand.

"No!" cried Kate. "Wait!"

Charlie swam, using up every last reserve of energy he had. He grabbed the German's belt, turned, and pulled him toward the human chain. The soldier moaned as Charlie shoved him forward. Kate reached out and grabbed him by the shoulder of his coat. Charlie saw her eyes bulge as she realized who she was saving . . .

A wave slapped him in the face. He swallowed half of it.

Charlie coughed and sputtered, feeling the ocean shove him. He wiped the salty water out of his eyes and saw that Kate and the rest of the chain were passing the German along . . . but they were suddenly so far away. He put his head down, pumped his arms and legs, and motored for the shore for a solid minute, until he couldn't take any more.

Then he raised his head again . . . and saw that he was even farther away.

Riptide.

Charlie felt panic close around his heart like a skeleton hand. A classic rip current—you didn't feel a thing until you were too far out, and the harder you swam for the shore, the farther it yanked you away. Suddenly, he was floating out near where the boat had wrecked, with huge oil fires burning on either side of him and bits and pieces of the wreckage floating all around him.

"HELP!" he cried, floundering his arms. He knew from the swim training they'd done at school that it was the wrong thing to do. He should be conserving his energy and trying to swim parallel to the current. But parallel meant swimming into a huge patch of burning oil, and he was already so tired . . . so tired . . .

Another wave hit him in the face. He inhaled salt water, coughed, spasmed. The water felt colder and colder around him.

He missed his mom. He wanted to go home.

As his vision began to go blurry, Charlie thought he saw a dark shape with glowing eyes in the water. He closed his eyes, and suddenly he was floating, warm, safe. He'd be home soon, a voice in his head told him, home with Mom and Dad and Kate. Even Buster would be there. He could almost feel the dog's fur beneath his hands now . . .

CHAPTER 22

JUNE 28, 1943
PALM BEACH, FLORIDA
10:40 P.M. LOCAL TIME

Buster didn't care that his skin burned. He didn't care that his nostrils were full of water, that there were other people calling out to him.

He paddled harder than he ever had. He clenched Charlie's shirt collar in his mouth like letting it go would kill him.

The *war* couldn't have this one.

There—Katie. She was part of another human leash, just like the one on the beach all those weeks ago. Her eyes went wide as she saw him, and she waved and called for Buster. Buster felt the current pulling at his fur once more, but this time, he knew what to do. He didn't try to swim to shore. He swam sideways until he was out of the current, outsmarting its pull. Then he could safely paddle to Katie.

Almost there . . .

NOW. Kate seized Charlie's arm and dragged him in. Then she grabbed Buster by his collar. She yelled back to the leash of people, and all at once they were all being pulled in, dragged to shore.

The minute he felt sand under his paws, Buster ran to where Charlie lay. A man, a sailor, knelt next to him, pressing on Charlie's chest with both his hands and breathing into Charlie's mouth. Buster had never felt more focused, more horribly in the moment, then he did right now.

The man pushed. He blew out Charlie's cheeks.

Nothing.

Buster whined. *No, no, no.*

He ran up next to Charlie and nuzzled his hand. Licked his fingers.

Please, Charlie. Please—

Charlie's eyes flew open. He lurched, turned,

and spat water onto the sand.

Buster barked for joy but felt tired all at once. He went and laid down next to Charlie, feeling the boy's hand find his ear. Buster let his human pet him, even as his skin stung from where the fire had touched him.

He was a good dog. He'd done all right.

CHAPTER 23

JULY 1, 1943
PALM BEACH, FLORIDA
1:37 P.M. LOCAL TIME

"More ice cream?" asked the woman in the blue SPARs uniform.

Kate put one hand to her stomach and held the other out to the officer. "I feel like I might pop," she said. By the time the woman turned to Charlie, he was already holding out his bowl for another helping. The woman gave him a grin and took his bowl to refill it.

They sat at a picnic table in the courtyard of their building, the whole area abuzz with uniformed personnel. A coast guardsman passed out burgers and hot dogs from a huge grill—a rare treat, brought together by people in the building pooling their ration cards. Women from Mom's Wave garrison and members of SPARs chatted and sipped drinks. In one corner, Hank and Miss Feng talked (flirtatiously close, Kate noted mentally). Occasionally one of the neighborhood kids—Mickey and Jeffrey recounting their night on the beach, or Siobhan Lerner pestering guardsmen about whether they'd ever punched a Nazi—caught sight of Charlie and Kate and waved. Red, white, and blue streamers hung all around the gate to the courtyard. At their center was a banner reading "CONGRATULATIONS, CHARLIE AND KATE!"

The twins' plot to foil the German invasion had become a huge deal around the neighborhood and had made the local press. The Rankin siblings and their friends were considered heroes by the *Palm Beach Post*, who ran sensational accounts of them foiling a plot to effectively cut Florida's supply routes off from the rest of the country. Vital stores of food, ammunition, and construction supplies would have never reached their

& KATE!

destination, and the war effort would have been effectively hobbled . . . if they hadn't intercepted that code from the Germans.

Even more important was the German officer Charlie had saved from drowning at the last minute. According to Hank, he was a high-ranking officer who defected as soon as he woke up in the hospital and gave the US government the names and locations of several similar invasion plots set to take place along the southern coast of the country.

Kate watched Hank chuckling at something Miss Feng said. He caught her eye and winked at her. Her face felt hot, and she smiled and looked away. No one was going to catch this hero blushing . . . but she was still happy she'd gotten a wink.

As the SPARs officer dropped off Charlie's fresh bowl of ice cream, Mom came up behind them, putting a hand on each of their shoulders. She looked extra-smart in her uniform today, Kate noticed, but she did her best to give them stern glares.

"Charlie, how many is this?" asked Mom.

"I'm not counting," said Charlie, and crammed

a spoonful of chocolate ice cream in his mouth.

"Whatever it is, that's the last one," she said. "You're still grounded for not telling me about what was happening, mister. Same for you, Katie."

"They're throwing us a party, Mom," said Kate, gesturing to the courtyard around them. "I think it all worked out in the end."

"You can think whatever you like," said Mom. "Next time, you tell me immediately."

"Next time we intercept Nazi espionage plans?" asked Kate.

"Next time *anything* risky happens, wiseacre," she said, tousling Kate's hair. "Have fun today. Tomorrow, chores become your life."

As she walked off, Charlie turned to Kate. "I could use a break," he said. "Want to go check on Buster, see if he wants to come down?"

"That sounds nice," said Kate.

They were on the third-floor stairs when a voice called out, "Young Rankins." Mr. Horowitz waited for them on the landing, hands in his pockets, a book of crosswords tucked under one arm.

"It appears," said Mr. Horowitz, "that your

message in the bottle turned out to be important after all."

Kate decided to own up to it. "We're sorry we lied to you, Mr. Horowitz."

The old man glanced over his shoulder and motioned for Kate to keep her voice down. "Hornby, Kate. If anyone in the building asks, I'm still just Mike Hornby, an old man with nothing to hide. Your government and I did a lot of work together to make sure I'm allowed my privacy. And it's quite all right. I suppose it's worth mentioning that I reached out to a few friends of my own after you left. They spoke to the prisoners at that POW camp, and they confessed to . . . tossing a few more bottles in the ocean, if you get my meaning."

His words struck Kate. "Is . . . is that why the coast guard cutter was out there? Did you contact them after talking to us?"

Mr. Horowitz shrugged. "Who's to say? What matters is, everything turned out all right." The older man turned to Charlie. "I'm also impressed you rescued that German, Charlie. I wouldn't have."

"It wasn't for him," said Charlie. "It was for me. I wanted to do the right thing."

Mr. Horowitz nodded slowly. "Fair enough, *kamarád*. I can't fault you for that. Now, if you'll excuse me, I have to make sure all these soldiers and sailors don't trample my garden." And with that, he turned down the stairs and walked off, his footsteps echoing behind him.

The twins went up to their apartment and tiptoed down the hall to Mom's room. Kate cracked the door and peeked in.

"They're still asleep," she said.

"Figures," whisper-laughed Charlie. "Buster becomes a war hero, and all he does is hang out with his famous girlfriend."

Buster snoozed at the foot of Mom's bed, breathing slow and steady. Around his middle was a tight weave of bandages, hiding the oil burns he'd gotten while swimming to rescue Charlie. Next to him lay a chocolate Labrador whose muscular frame looked especially stark next to Buster. She lay as though sleeping, but her eyes darted up when Kate had peeked in the door. She looked so alert that Kate had no doubt she could spring into action at any moment.

Skipper, the hero dog of Pearl Harbor. Kate remembered Dad reading them the stories from the newspaper, about a dog who had helped a member of the mess hall crew save countless sailors on the sinking USS *West Virginia*. Marcus Dean had opened doors for black people in the navy, while his trusted companion, Skipper, a brave Labrador, had led the way for the army's dog soldier program. She'd been out on dozens of naval missions, had saved over fifty lives . . . and now she was here, lying next to Buster.

Kate turned to say something to Charlie about how she couldn't believe Buster had become a hero . . . but her brother was gone.

She found him in the kitchen, turning Dad's binoculars over in his hands. A spark of panic lit up inside her, seeing the boy who'd just eaten four-and-a-quarter bowls of ice cream (she *had* been counting) holding their father's binocs. She gasped—and Charlie looked up suddenly.

The binoculars leaped from his hands and hit the floor with a crack. Glass spilled out of one lens and onto the floor. Charlie clapped his hand to his mouth.

"Aw, Kate, you were right," he stammered. His eyes went red, and fat tears spilled down his cheeks. "I did it. I ruined them. I'm so sorry. This makes two of Dad's things I've destroyed now. I'm such an idiot."

Kate looked down at the broken binoculars and up at her crying brother . . . and realized she cared way more about the second thing than the first. She'd almost lost Charlie—how could she possibly be worried about losing some object?

She threw her arms around Charlie and pulled him close. After a moment, he hugged her back.

"It's okay," she said into his shoulder. "It's just a thing. They break sometimes. What's important is us. We're all that matters. Dad would understand that."

Charlie squeezed her tightly. "I think he'd be really proud of us," he whispered.

Kate felt a sob rip through her. "I do too," she whispered.

The twins stood there in the silent kitchen hugging each other. They'd lost so much, and had so far to go . . . but Kate had her brother, and he'd always have her. They had their mom, their friends, their loyal dog . . . it was amazing how lucky they were.

They'd get through the rest of the war together. At the end of the day, there was no greater victory than that.

BATTLE FACTS

World War II's biggest battles were fought on foreign soil. But at home in America, there was still plenty of hardship, victory, and danger.

What was life like in the US during World War II?
World War II was a time of hard work and sacrifice for people living in the United States. Supplies were scarce, and almost all raw materials were being used to aid the military. That meant nothing could go to waste—rubber, aluminum, paper, all of it went to the war effort. There was also constant news of battles and casualties coming home from the war abroad. All of this led to a sense of worry around the United States.

Human labor was also a valuable resource during wartime. Because most working-age men were fighting abroad, women had to take over a lot of the day-to-day jobs usually reserved for men. For the first time in American history, women were working in factories, writing for newspapers, and even patrolling the streets as police or military employees.

How did the coast guard defend American shores?

The coast guard was a vital part of defending America at home during World War II. Coast guardsmen patrolled beaches around vital locations in the United States—harbors where supplies were delivered and military ships landed. They served as both transport and rescue both for soldiers that needed to be delivered to specific locations and those who were stuck out at sea. Their use of small ships and amphibious craft—water-borne ships that could also make their way up on shore—made them uniquely helpful.

What were U-boats?

U-boats—an English term for the German word *Unterseeboot* ("under-sea boat")—were German submarines used in World Wars I and II. U-boats were quick, quiet, and powerful, and American ships before the Allies knew they were there. Winston Churchill, England's prime minister during World War II, once said that the only thing that really frightened him in the war was "the U-boat peril."

25

TIMELINE OF

September 1, 1939
Germany invades Poland; war breaks out in Europe

September 1939
Battle of the Atlantic begins

1939

1940

September 1940
London Blitz begins

September 1940
US government begins the draft

1941

May 1941
End of London Blitz

December 7, 1941
Attack on Pearl Harbor

December 8, 1941
US enters war

December 8 to December 10, 1941
First Battle of Guam: Japanese forces capture the Pacific Island

1942

January 1942
Dogs for Defense program is founded

June 1942
Operation Pastorius

July 1942
US government commits to use of trained war dogs

August 1942
US begins work on atomic bomb

WORLD WAR II

1943

September 1943
Italian forces surrender

1944

June 6, 1944
D-Day at Normandy in France

July 21, 1944 to August 8, 1944
Second Battle of Guam: US takes control from Japan

August 25, 1944
Paris is freed from German control

1945

May 1945
Battle of the Atlantic ends

May 7, 1945
German forces surrender

May 8, 1945
V-E Day (Victory in Europe)

August 6, 1945
Atomic bomb dropped on Hiroshima

August 9, 1945
Atomic bomb dropped on Nagasaki

August 14, 1945
Japanese forces surrender

September 2, 1945
V-J Day (Victory in Japan), Japanese sign surrender agreement

MEET A REAL HERO DOG

SINBAD

US COAST GUARD HERO DOG

NATIONALITY: AMERICAN

BREED: MUTT

JOB: CHIEF DOG

STRENGTHS: BRAVERY, INTELLIGENCE, BOOSTING MORALE

TRAINING: ON THE JOB

STATIONED: USCCC *CAMPBELL*

HEROIC MOMENT: PROTECTING THE CREW OF HIS SHIP AFTER IT WAS RAMMED BY A U-BOAT

HONORS: AMERICAN DEFENSE SERVICE MEDAL, AMERICAN CAMPAIGN MEDAL, EUROPEAN-AFRICAN-MIDDLE-EASTERN CAMPAIGN MEDAL, ASIATIC-PACIFIC CAMPAIGN MEDAL, WORLD WAR II VICTORY MEDAL, AND NAVY OCCUPATION SERVICE MEDAL

HOME FRONT Q&A

What were the Waves and SPARs?

During World War II, several military branches created women's reserves to help with emergency services and military operations at home. The navy's military reserve was called Wave (Women Accepted for Volunteer Emergency service), while the coast guard's was called SPAR (short for the coast guard's Latin motto *Semper Paratus*, meaning "Always ready"). The Waves and SPARs provided vital services on the home front, both in running war drives for raw materials and in providing emergency services like driving ambulances and aiding nurses.

What was life in Florida like during World War II?

Floridians had an especially tough time during World War II. Florida's location and geography, jutting out into the Atlantic Ocean at the southeast edge of the country, meant that it was right in the middle of navy engagements with German U-boats. Sometimes, residents in Florida could see flashes of light in the distance from navy battles, or smoke from marine vessels.

On top of that, Florida's role as a tourist hub made it a dangerous place during the war. It took significant effort to convince beachfront resort owners to aid the war effort or turn their hotels into barracks for naval officers and coast guardsmen. Meanwhile, several famous Europeans who were used to spending their winters at resorts in Palm Beach and Miami suddenly found themselves being interrogated or barred from entry.

What were victory gardens?

Victory gardens were agricultural gardens run by citizens in the United States to help feed citizens during wartime. Due to the shortage of food caused by the war, the government began urging Americans to grow their own vegetable gardens. Pamphlets were written and given out to Americans on how to grow and garden their own produce everywhere from front lawns to window boxes.

Why were Asian Americans treated with suspicion during World War II?

After Pearl Harbor, suspicion of Japanese Americans spread throughout the country. The thought was that all people of Japanese descent were secretly in league with the Empire of Japan. It didn't matter whether or not a person had been born in the United States—looking Japanese was enough. This quickly became a widespread paranoia about all Asian Americans, and eventually led to the internment of Japanese Americans in camps. This was, of course, shameful and racist, but at the time, it was the panicked government's perceived solution to a fear of sabotage from within America.

Were there really POW camps in the US?

There were indeed. Once the United States entered the war, the British government asked America to help them house prisoners. Over 400,000 Germans lived in 700 POW camps across the United States, mostly along the East Coast and in the south. In fact, many Germans were happy to be captured by the Americans—American POW camps were well kept, and most Germans would rather be caught by anyone other than the Soviets, whose prisons were famous for their cruelty.

The US government focused American paranoia on the immigrants caught up in the national security dragnet that swept both coasts. Within a few months after Pearl Harbor, the FBI arrested 264 Italian Americans, nearly 1,400 German Americans, and over 2,200 Japanese Americans. Many were never shown evidence leading to their arrest. Beyond those initial arrests, however, came a much heavier cost. Throughout the war, approximately 100,000 Japanese Americans were forced into internment camps, and 50,000 Italian Americans were similarly relocated.

Why would German POWs be treated more fairly than Japanese Americans?

The sad fact is that German prisoners were white Europeans, and plenty of Americans had German relatives. Asian Americans, meanwhile, were visibly different from the majority of people in the country, and therefore had an extra level of prejudice leveled against them.

Why were there blackouts in America?

Blackouts were organized dimming and dousing of lights during World War II. The idea of a blackout was to make coastal cities less visible targets for planes or submarines attacking at night. Blackouts were maintained by air raid wardens who would patrol the streets, urging Americans to close their drapes, turn out their lights, and put out any fires they might have burning. These were especially useful in hiding the coasts and population centers in Florida, whose location and use as a resort state made it basically a landing strip for anyone approaching the United States over or under the Atlantic.

Did German spies ever invade America?

Yes, and especially in coastal areas like New York, Massachusetts, Virginia, and Florida. There are numerous cases of U-boats sending Germans, some with American citizenship, in as spies in the US to sabotage supply routes. In fact, white supremacists in America have even honored these dead Nazi spies with public memorials. The most famous of these spy operations was Operation Pastorius.

What was Operation Pastorius?

Operation Pastorius was a failed German infiltration of the United States in 1942. The Nazis sent a series of German soldiers to America with the mission of destroying strategic targets on American soil, including hydroelectric plants, railroad passages, and aluminum factories.

Under cover of night, German submarines sent soldiers on shore in locations in New York and Florida. The spies arrived wearing German navy uniforms, so if they were arrested they would be charged as enemy combatants rather than spies. Once on shore, the Florida and New York teams were to change into civilian clothes, buy train tickets, and make their way to rendezvous points. The Florida teams bought train tickets to Cincinnati, but then split up, with two going to Chicago and two to New York. The team that landed in Long Island headed to New York.

But they got stopped at the beach by the coast guard, right?

Nope. The German soldiers infiltrated American soil. They encountered one coast guardsman, but they bribed him with enough money to leave them alone.

Wait, the spies *made it*? Then how did the mission fail?

From within. The story goes that mission head George Dasch called his partner, Ernst Berger, into his hotel room. Dasch revealed that he hated Nazi Germany and wanted to defect. Berger immediately agreed, and the two men gave up the mission to the FBI. Funnily enough, when Dasch called the FBI, no one believed him at first—he had to literally go to the Bureau's offices and turn himself in.

Okay, what do you do if you get stuck in a rip current?

In the story, Buster learned quickly that if he tried to fight the current and swim toward shore, he'd only get sucked farther out into the ocean. But when he swam parallel to the shore, he eventually made his way out of the current. Then he could swim safely toward the sand.

Join the Fight!

DON'T MISS THE NEXT
ACTION-PACKED MISSION

PROLOGUE

May 22nd, 1941, 4:52 a.m.

Julio's heart hammered in his chest.

The bridge and the wheelhouse, where Captain Bayne stood every day guiding the *Susquehanna* and her crew, were completely gone. Smoke billowed from below deck. Cannons thundered in the distance.

Julio froze with panic. He knew the merchant marine ship had been hit at least twice by German U-boat torpedoes. Any second, they could be hit by another one—the one that could sink the ship.

The ship's whistle sounded two long blasts followed by a short one. The signal for distress.

"Captain Bayne must still be alive, Jack," Julio said to his dog. "Everything will be okay."

No answering bark.

Julio looked behind him. No Jack.

He looked on either side. No Jack.

"Jack!" Julio shouted above the noise. "Jack!"

Julio's heart froze with fear. Where was his dog?

Someone bumped into him. Spud Campbell, the third cook, stumbled past Julio, his eyes wide and uncomprehending.

Julio grabbed Spud's arm. "Have you seen Jack?"

Spud looked at him like he was a total stranger. He pulled his arm from Julio's grasp. "They're gone," he said, shaking his head. And then, before Julio could ask who "them" was, Spud hurried away.

An explosion in the engine room shook the ship hard. Julio was thrown to the deck.

"No!" Julio cried. He staggered to his feet. Maybe Jack was waiting for him at their lifeboat. Jack was smart. He'd know what to do that if they got separated, wouldn't he?

Julio stared in disbelief. No Jack. No lifeboat. Just a tangle of useless ropes. And the lifeboats on the other side of the ship were gone.

The *Susquehanna* lurched and tilted to one side like a wounded animal.

Julio's blood turned to ice. He had to find Jack and get off the boat. It was sinking fast!

Suddenly, Julio heard a familiar bark.

"Jack!" the boy cried. "Where are you?"

Smoke billowed up through the large forward

hatch cover. He heard a splash.

"Jack!"

He ran to the starboard side. A hole big enough to drive a supply truck through had been blown into the side, exactly where the engine room was. Water poured into the ship.

In the sea below, a lifeboat full of crew rowed frantically away from the *Susquehanna*.

"Hey!" Julio called, waving his arms. "Hey! Don't leave us!"

The face of Sarge, the ship's bosun, looked up at him. Sarge was the boss of the ordinary and able seamen. He'd tell them to wait for him.

"There's another lifeboat on the port side," Sarge called. "Get it down and get away from the ship as quick as you can!"

"But it was—"

"We'll look for you, Julio, but we've got to get away from the ship. She's sinking fast!"

Julio leaned as far as he dared over the side of the boat and watched in horror as his only hope rowed away.

Read them all!